Screwloose
Conversations with
Screwtape

Images on the book cover are an "Ouroboros" encircling the "Eye of Horus".

SCREWLOOSE CONVERSATIONS WITH SCREWTAPE

Don Goh

PARTRIDGE
A Penguin Random House Company

To order additional copies of this book, contact
Toll Free 800 101 2657 (Singapore)
Toll Free 1 800 81 7340 (Malaysia)
orders.singapore@partridgepublishing.com

www.partridgepublishing.com/singapore

CONTENTS

Part 1

Part 2

"The thin line between fact and fiction is belief."

PART 1

PART 1

PROLOGUE

Hello to all,

I am still slightly confused as I am not too sure if this is the end or the beginning of my stories. But thank you, all the same, for being willing to read my stories. However I do need to let you know that I am most probably lying most of the time. Yes, I admit it, I am a liar.

A liar either by nature or via preternatural influence. But either way it is all the same. I am still a liar.

If you think I mirror someone, it is actually Neil Gaiman. One of the most capable and celebrated writers around. Why he admits to being a liar I am unsure, as I do not know him personally, but the above are my reasons.

Another writer of note is John Barth. Very postmodern and who had influenced me with his own work of "Chimera".

Also of note is Universalism. A form of Theology.

It is important that I tell you all these as they would heavily affect the way in which you read my stories. So please pardon my rambling.

Also, pardon my confusion, if this is the beginning you are advised that it is a must to read the stories in numerical order. But if this is the end then please read the stories in reverse numerical order. Either way it should result in a form of back masking. Hopefully making the stories more devilishly diabolic.

Like my stories or hate them. Think through them or throw them aside like rubbish. It is your choice, as a reader, in exercising your free-will. As for me my only wish as a liar is that you are able to enjoy them. I suppose most good lies are that way. If you cannot enjoy them they are probably bad lies. Bad in the sense that they make you want to vomit.

So sorry if you dirty your carpet or just simply felt like you just wasted your time reading my stories.

My humble apologies.

[Makes a curtsy as best as I can]

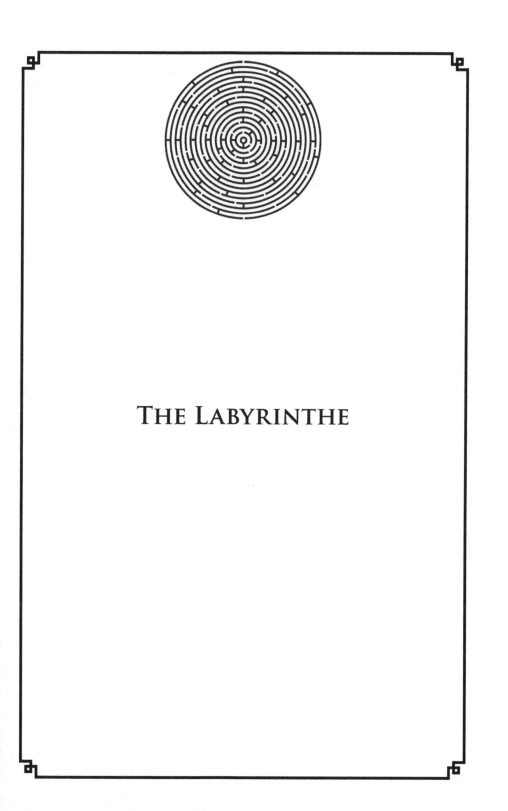

THE LABYRINTHE

FOREWORD

Hope is one of the greatest gifts which mankind has. It is the thing that shines forth to provide us the strength to move on even when placed in the direst of circumstances. Hope is what tells us, despite the hard facts facing us, that there is still a solution to the problem. Hope is what enables us to face the unknown.

But what happens when that hope leads us onto a path, which we can never extract ourselves from and this path irrevocably leads us further away from the very things that gives us meaning, joy and *hope*.

This story is a tribute to horror and an author of horror who wrote the following quote.

"The oldest and strongest emotion of mankind is fear, and the oldest and strongest kind of fear is fear of the unknown." H.P. Lovecraft, *Author of the Cthulhu Mythos*

"Your hypothesis seems sound but your proofs and experimental data still require more work." Sighed the Professor.

"Not to worry though, what you have would still be good enough for your thesis submission but if you are going to make it for your scholarship application you definitely need more work."

The student then earnestly replied. "I have been working on it for a year and there is just too much data to process. Furthermore my hypothesis for the GUT is something off the mainstream theories - although I think it does show promise – but the data that needs to be crunched is just too daunting."

"I too think it is worth looking further into and since you are applying for the scholarship might as well go all the way. After all, once you are done with everything you probably would be getting your PhD." The Professor smiled assuringly.

"Thanks for the optimism." The student smiled back grudgingly.

The Professor's room was a quaint office typical of any University's professor. It had a window facing a wide green field interlaced with paths leading to various parts of the University. The paths were lined with maple trees which provide not only shade but color to the plain field as the autumn season approaches.

The pale late afternoon sun illuminated the room which was mainly filled with books on various subjects related to theoretical physics, with a small corner at the bottom of the long four tiered shelf, occupied by books on Natural Philosophy. In front of the shelf is a single drawer desk with a laptop and various stationary on top of it. Under the desk is a roller cabinet with three compartments. Towards the opposite end of the room was another four tiered shelf and a critically damped heavy wooden door, on the right, which leads to the common hallway.

The Professor and student were seated on a couch leaning just below the window. The Professor slowly handed over the thesis which he had just read through and smiled encouragingly before pointing to the shelves near the door.

"Look at the various puzzles and trinkets which I have placed on the shelves. You have played with some of them and would have found that some are quite challenging."

The student nodded in agreement.

"However, each and every one of them has a solution and with time and patience the solution can be found. Therefore I believe that, even though I am not a man of faith, the same goes for your problem. No need to worry or be anxious, I am sure the University would be more than willing to help. You could probably work on campus while you sort out your hypothesis before submitting it in for a scholarship application. Give it about two years and with what I understand about your capabilities you should be ready by then."

The student turned back and looked at the Professor with an appreciative sweet smile and just sighed.

*****

There were two children in the room. The room was a playroom with toys littering the ground and a low cabinet for storing children's books. The children were playing with Lego bricks, building what looked like fortifications for their medieval knight figurines. They were enthusiastically discussing about the next grand adventure they were going to undertake.

The boy exclaimed.

"I am going to build a laby...rin." (The boy was trying to pronounce the word labyrinth.)

"Like those mazes we get to do in those puzzle books which mom got us. I will make it so hard you will find it difficult to find a way out of it."

The girl, who was taller than the boy by half-a-head, then retorted.

"Don't think you can do that. The ones in the puzzle books are always so easy. Unless you also place some scary monster in it, to make it more difficult, like the story which mom read us the night before."

"You mean the story about the minotaur? Hmm… Then I shall place a dragon inside the maze to gobble up your hero." The boy said menacingly.

"That would probably make it more interesting but my hero's going to win anyway like the guy in the story and your dragon is going to be killed by my magic sword."

"My dragon can breathe fire… Rahhh." Roared the boy.

"I have my magic shield." The girl snapped while the boy just stuck out his tongue.

The boy then continued to build his maze while the girl looked around for other things to add to the maze.

Suddenly the girl exclaimed.

"I know! Why don't you place a treasure chest inside the maze? My hero can then enter the maze to find the treasure chest. Anyway I think dragons always have treasure chests or something really precious with them."

"That would be a great idea!"

Now the boy was ever more eager to build his intricate maze and excitedly went back to it.

Then there was a knock on the door to the playroom and the doorknob turned. The children's heads turned towards the door as the door opened slowly to reveal a lady with straight golden hair that flowed slightly beyond the shoulders and curled slightly at the ends. She was wearing a white apron over a plain turquoise shirt, beige colored pants and dark colored slippers.

The children then shouted in unison. "Mom!"

The lady smiled at her two children.

"Its time for dinner and your dad is going to be back soon so please be ready."

"So soon? Looks like I won't be able to finish my maze." The boy sulked.

"Don't worry I will help you. Then we can let daddy try to see if he can figure his way out!" The girl reassured him.

The lady then grinned and said "Alright. I will call you all down once dad is home."

The children grinned back and excitedly went back to building their maze.

The lady closed back the door and went back downstairs to hang up her apron.

The lady was about mid-forties while her children were two years apart with the oldest being ten years of age. The house was a modest two-story house in a quiet neighborhood situated near the University where her husband works. They had just moved in about two years ago when her husband decided to take the teaching assignment in the University. The pay was good and the University had the relevant facilities for her husband to continue his research. She helps take care of the house and the children and is thankful that there is an elementary school situated nearby. That was also one of the main reasons which made the move easier.

The sun was almost setting outside and the porch light was already on.

The sound of a car was heard rolling in the driveway and a car door slammed shut. The dinner table was already set so the lady called to her children upstairs. Hearing a muffled reply she went on to the front door of the house.

Just as she was reaching the door, it opened and the professor entered holding his briefcase.

She smiled.

"Let me help you with your coat and hat."

"Thanks. Anything in the mail?"

"Yes. Its on the living room table. The children should be on their way down soon."

*****

The children had finished their meal just as their Dad was about to leave the dining table. They hurried upstairs excitedly to finish up their labyrinth while their Dad went off to the living room to await their challenge. Mom was clearing up the dishes from the dining table and placing them neatly in the dishwasher.

The professor made his way to the living room table and sat down on a couch beside it. He went on to grab the letters which were on the table and sieved through them. One of the envelopes caught his eye. It was a cream colored small envelope with an intricately designed stamp marked on its sealed end. He stared at it and immediately recognized it to be the stamp of the *Ghost Club*.

The *Ghost Club* was a side hobby of his which he was a part of ever since his University days. Seeing it brought a light smile to his face.

The club was mainly a boys club and its interest was in paranormal activity. They would dig up tales and legends and go sniffing around abandoned buildings or cemeteries to check out if these stories were true. Most of them probably did not even believe any of the stories they dug up but they all thought it was something fun and exciting. They sometimes even joked about probably getting a Nobel Prize if they ever discovered a real ghost.

He opened up the envelope and found a piece of paper addressed to him and it read:

Dear John,

Its been a long time since we last met and understand that you are busy and stuff but we heard that you moved and coincidentally we just discovered this interesting location near your town. So we were thinking if you would be interested to have a reunion at your University pub? Many of us would be gathering there for old time's sake so really hope that you can be there. If you are free, meet us fourteen days later at 7pm.

Cheers,
Ralf

P.s. – Enclosed within is also a write-up on this location that I have found. Hope we get a Nobel this time.

He smile again at the letter.

Ah… good old Ralf. One of his best friends.

They still kept in contact occasionally via email but seldom met up as they were working in different states. Interesting that he should send a letter with their club's official stamp.

Although *he was* one of their club's *most avid* enthusiasts.

He must have found something really interesting and thought probably this would be a good chance for them to meet up again.

Fourteen days later… That would be the following Friday night after counting from the letter's date. The professor flipped out his smart phone to check his calendar.

Nothing on. The professor grinned and keyed the appointment into his calendar.

Then he unfolded another piece of paper from the envelope and began to read the write-up, which was typed out and photocopied for mass sending.

Dear friends,

I have happened to chance upon an interesting location near John Strandson's place. It's a bit hard to tell you the location now but once we meet up I can direct you all there. It is this cemetery, which according to local history, was once an open field that belonged to a rich man's estate.

Within this field resides a really large maze which was built for his own personal pleasure. But apparently the estate was subsequently abandoned and is now owned by the state. They apparently decided to build a cemetery around the maze. Not very sure why, however numerous legends abound with regard to this maze. It seems that the maze itself has as numerous names as its legends.

Here are some of the names I found – Maze of Death, Maze of Demons, Maze of Attrition, Labyrinthe... and many more. Think you get the point. Sounds spooky but some records suggest that the guy who had the maze built was slightly eccentric and has an immense interest in chess competitions. He probably built the maze as some sort of challenge for his guests and initially named it "Labyrinthe Diabolique".

It was recorded somewhere that he once boasted about it being the most complicated maze ever built. As you can probably observe from the names I have listed the rich man was probably well tolerated by the normal folk around.

Some of the legends state that after the estate opened up, people who have tried to challenge the maze at night have actually gone missing. Its like the people never got out of the maze and were never seen again thereafter.

Sound interesting yet? Hope to have piqued your gray matter. I think it's definitely worth a visit! Hope to see you guys at the reunion.

It definitely sounded interesting for the professor. Sort of an added bonus to the gathering. It probably would be good to relive old times and it was also the first time he ever heard about this local mystery. It was probably more vibrant among the older local folks.

Seems like its going to be an interesting reunion.

*****

The University pub was a small establishment. It had a bar counter with a rather assorted alcoholic menu and it had a kitchen which served finger food and some easy to cook meals like fish & chips and Maryland chicken. Its seating space was situated outside of its premises on an open lawn. So come evening it would switch on its strings of carnival-like multi-colored light bulbs that were stringed on the tall trees sheltering the lawn.

But tonight was a full moon on an almost cloudless sky so the lawn was especially bright.

It was already about 9pm. John and his friends all arrived pretty punctually. They were all surprised that they could all still recognize each other. Altogether there were ten of them, minus two from the old team who were not able to make it. They had found themselves two large benches, placed side by side, then proceeded to ordering food and chatted until now.

Most of them were married, except Ralf and Dean, and all were properly employed. They were all happy to be able to reunite after all these years. John especially thanked Ralf for successfully organizing this gathering.

Ralf suddenly stood up and with a raised voice said "Alright everyone! It has been nice catching up with all of you but are you now ready for the main course of tonight's gathering?"

Everyone then looked at him and shouted "Yea!"

"So how are we going to get to this graveyard of yours?" Asked Sam.

"Coming to that!" Ralf replied enthusiastically.

"I have brought with me several tourist maps and marked out the route which we are going to take."

Ralf then gave out the maps for everyone to share.

"Not to worry about getting lost, as we would be moving in a convoy which should not be a problem in this town's quiet streets." Ralf gave John a knowing wink.

Ah Ralf, thought John.

"Always the meticulous one in the club, looking after every detail possible in every one of our escapades."

Everyone started looking at the maps and once done gave a knowing nod towards Ralf.

Ralf then continued to brief. "The graveyard isn't far from here but after scouting the location this afternoon I would suggest that we take three vehicles instead as there isn't enough parking space outside the cemetery gate. Are you all ok with that?"

All nodded their heads in agreement.

"Alright! Any questions?"

All shook their heads.

"Then once we are done with our round of drinks let us set off on our night of adventure! Don't forget to bring along any gear you might have brought along!" Ralf grinned.

*****

The large iron gate of the cemetery was made of caste iron and it had an intricate design woven into its ironwork. The boundaries of the cemetery were iron grills that were slightly taller than an average man's height. Looking beyond its iron protection, its pathways were observed to be lined with crooked trees, which gave an ominous feel to the place as their dark shadowy branches looked like crooked hands that might reach down upon any passerby.

Even though the full moon helped illuminate the pathways for anyone passing through, it also made the cemetery's foreboding presence more greatly felt as the tombstones and their accompanying gothic architecture were made more visible.

They had parked their cars along the roadway just outside the iron gate. With their gear gathered they were standing in front of the gate, pausing to gaze pass it into the area of no return.

They looked at each other and smiled. *Just like old times.*

Ralf then motioned for them to huddle. Whispering softly.

"Alright. Just to check before we make our way in, everyone have their thermal cameras?" All nodded.

"Remember to place it properly so that we can capture whatever is in front of you. Sound recorder?" All nodded again.

"Same thing, place it where we can record what you hear. Handphone batteries full? If not, I brought spare walkie-talkies for communicating, in case you get lost, and also for easy tracking of your whereabouts." Suddenly there was doubtful mumbling.

"Oh, I brought my laptop and gear for this." Then everyone muttered in understanding and nodded.

Everyone was prepared.

"Then let's go."

Ralf led them to a small gateway built into the side of the large iron gate. It was not locked so everyone made their way through and switched on their torches. All of them were keeping deadly silent as Ralf then led them on a path towards the legendary labyrinth.

As they walked, they could hear the gravel crunching beneath their soles and the night air began to grow cooler as mist began to gather. The cemetery was surprisingly large from what they could observe as they traveled. It took them about an hour to reach their destination, at a leisurely pace. As they approached the end of their walk they saw a tall iron arch with two stone statues guarding its dark entrance which was about the width of two persons.

They walked closer to the arch and shined their torches on it. The statue on the left was a Unicorn rearing on its two hind legs while the statue on the right was a lion with its right front leg lifted up as it seemingly stared intently at anyone who was seeking to enter the arch. The top of the arch, also made of iron, was intricately patterned with what seems to be a sunburst symbol in the middle. Lining the two sides of the arch behind the statues was a stone wall that barricaded the length of the labyrinth. They shined their torches to the sides but were unable to make out where the stone walls ended.

Just as John walked forward to inspect the statues he felt a cold draft wafting out of the dark entrance under the arch. The stonework on the two statues were indeed detailed and of a high quality. Upon closer inspection of the stone walls it seems that they were also well laid with vines creeping along its rough surface.

Ralf was now unpacking all his gear, which he carried with him in a medium size sling bag. He took out his laptop and portable spare power supply. He also set up other electronic equipment for the receiving of signals from their cameras and handphones.

Everyone else also started to put on their gear and made sure they were properly placed.

John also walked back to the group and followed suite.

After Ralf had finished setting up his stuff they started testing their equipment with Ralf's. Once this was done, Ralf then softly asked them to gather around him.

"Now that we are set to go, allow me to brief you that beyond the archway is a big lawn or perhaps you might call it a garden but walk all the way down and you will find a long wall. Built into it are altogether nine archways which are nine entrances into the maze. I am not sure which of the nine would lead you to the exit or it could be that only one of them is the correct one but that, gentlemen, is one of the reasons why you all are here tonight as well." Ralf grinned with glee in the moonlight.

"So even if we do not get a Nobel prize at least we would have conquered this maze."

Everyone started to look at each other with a knowing grin, everyone hoping in their hearts to be able to conquer the maze. Apparently they also realized that they had just enough people tonight to accomplish this task.

"Alrighty. Let's get on with it then!" Pierced Ralf's loud voice through the night.

"And as an encouragement I have got an ice-box filled with cold beer, in the boot of my car, when we get back."

Everyone cheered, their voices ringing as they marched off towards the maze entrance.

*****

Upon entering the garden beyond the maze's entrance, with the illumination of the full moon and their nine torches they were able to make out a huge garden – the long wall at the opposite end was about 20 meters away – from what they were able to make out of the silhouette, which the top edge of the wall made and its length was probably about double the breath of the garden.

In between they were able to make out dark patches of groves or bushes, which were probably once adorned with flowers and in the middle was what looked like a tall dark shadow of a large tree. With the emptiness, interspersed between them, probably being pathways.

Dean then whispered. "I think the real start of the maze starts at the opposite end. Think we should stick together and find a way to the opposite end".

Everyone nodded in agreement and began their way forward, negotiating the meandering pathways by trying to maintain a general forward direction.

About fifteen minutes later they managed to find their way to the opposite end of the garden. Upon exiting the pathway they were on they reached a long wide corridor in front of the long wall. Shining their torches in front they found a rather tall stone wall and an entryway just in front of them. The entryway, as Ralf described, was an archway built into the stone wall and was framed by inlaid stonework.

Seeing that they have reached the start of the maze Dean began to take charge.

"I believe we should be at the center of the wall. So if four of us fanned out on each side we would be able to cover all the nine archways." Everyone muttered in agreement.

"Each one then stick to an archway and wave your torches towards my direction when you have found one. I will then make a count and when all eight of your torches are waving at me I will then signal with my torch for each side to move forward. How about that?"

All muttered in agreement again.

They then set off, four on each side.

John went with the right side and volunteered to move to the last archway since his torch was among the brighter ones.

After finding the third archway down the right side, it was observed that all the archways they have passed were similar in construction to Dean's.

John continued to walk alone along the wall to locate the fourth archway where upon finding it he shined his torch further down the right side and was able to see the outline of the top edge of the garden's side wall. Concluding that he had reached the last archway he then turned around and waved his torch in Dean's direction.

A few minutes later he received a message from Dean on his mobile phone inquiring if he had found an archway.

John smiled and replied "Yes".

Later he received a reply "All have found an archway. Pls proceed."

John then looked in Dean's direction and saw a torch waving them forward. Then with excitement and trepidation John shined his torch into the dark archway and proceeded into the labyrinth.

*****

Since Ralf received the message from Dean, informing that they were entering the maze, it's been already five hours. None of them have exited from the maze yet. He has been keeping track of them via his laptop all this while and had lost all electronic contact with them about an hour ago.

He first began to lose their video feeds, probably due to distance. Then he tried contacting them with his mobile phone but found that he was unable to connect through, which probably meant that the phone network was weak in the maze. This also probably meant that they were already deep into the maze and should be coming out soon.

Ralf then took a sip of coffee out of a thermos which he had brought with him. He then laid on the camping mat he was on and looked at the stars above. It was sure getting boring for him out here.

*****

John's wife Martha was up making breakfast for the children when she received a knock on her front door. She turned off the stove, wiping her hands on her apron, before proceeding to open the front door. Upon opening the door she saw a man with unkempt black hair, wearing a black jacket over a plain green shirt and jeans. Behind the man stood two police officers. The man in front of the door was sobbing with tears running down his face.

"Sorry... So very sorry. I..."

"Sorry? What has happened and who might you be?"

The man then softly replied "I am Ralf. John's friend."

Then a realization suddenly dawned upon Martha. Its been more than a day since John went out on Friday night to meet his old friends. Today's Sunday morning and there was still no sign of John. She had just assumed that he was probably still with his friends. After all it has been a long while since they last met and managed to gather together despite living in different states.

"John… Somethings happened to John?"

"Yes." Ralf was still sniffing.

"He… he has gone missing."

Martha then placed a hand over her mouth in shock.

"I have tried all I could to find him and the rest but I just could not find them. I even called in the police but we still could not find them."

"How did they go missing?" Martha exclaimed.

"We just decided to wander into an old maze situated inside an old town cemetery but I… I did not think that they would go missing." Sobbed Ralf.

"You mean they just went missing in the maze? Have you searched the whole area?"

"Yes we have… but we still cannot find them. We tried calling their mobile phones countless of times but nothing got through. We just got a tone indicating no reception."

This time the full realization of what just transpired hit Martha and her knees started to tremble before she fainted.

*****

John had been trying to find his way around the maze for almost forever. He was already quite tired and was also feeling slightly anxious. He looked at his watch, almost five hours has past, and when he looked up to find the moon he was unable to find it as the walls of the narrow stone wall passageways of the maze were too high. Although the moon's illuminating light could still be felt.

Labyrinthe Diabolique... This maze is beginning to feel diabolically endless.

He wondered how the others were doing? He had forgotten to bring along a water bottle and his throat was getting quite parched. As he stumbled along another intersection he began to wonder if he had passed here before but the stone walled passageways all looked the same. However he was not a person to give up easily, especially when faced with such puzzling challenges. He decided to try a right turn.

He had tried to contact Ralf earlier on his mobile phone but only received a tone for no reception.

Well. What's the worse that could happen? At the very most Ralf would get a search team in to find us. Thought John.

John continued to trudge on and when he made a sharp turn into what he thought would be another narrow passageway he was surprised to find himself entering a fairly small open area framed by four walls with no other exit apart from where he just came in.

This is new.

Light mist filled the area. In the middle was a rectangular stone base where when he shined his torch on it revealed what looks like a stone table or altar. At its side there were stone carvings woven onto the stone surface. He shined his torch around the other parts of the square room and found that there was nothing else except for the stone base.

He walked closer to inspect the stone base. Upon closer inspection he found that there seemed to be some writings on the top of the stone base which were covered by moss and soil.

He reached out to try and wipe away what was obscuring the writings when suddenly he felt breathing behind him. It sounded heavy and strangely he could even feel a waft of cold air tingling behind his neck.

Then a deep hollow voice spoke "What do you seek?"

John's hairs were beginning to stand. He was staring into space as he slowly turned around. When he had finally finished turning he stared ahead and saw a dark figure blocking the entrance from where he had entered.

Mists curled around the figure and where he stood there was little illumination from the moon. John was tempted to bring up his torch but he decided against it. He was, however, able to make out a silhouette of what looked like a stocky human figure. Yet there was something on its head which looked like horns.

The figure then asked again, more insistently this time "What do you seek?"

John was too terrified to answer.

"Do you seek treasure? Knowledge? Power?" The figure paused slightly between each subject.

"What do you seek?"

There was a moment of still silence. Then John slowly muttered "None… But what… do you offer?"

After a moments pause. The figure answered. "I offer a choice."

John quivering slightly at the answer then spoke "What choice?"

The figure then moved forward and with the moon's slight illumination revealing a bull's head set upon a muscular human torso.

A minotaur! John suddenly cringed back towards the stone base.

"You have entered the Labyrinth. You can no longer leave. You may only choose. You can choose to become a part of the labyrinth or you may choose to continue to wander it."

"You must now choose."

The words echoed in John's mind. *You can no longer leave... It cannot be! This must be a nightmare... a dream.* Martha and his children flashed through his mind. *My family... and friends...*

YANKIKOVICH THE CLOWN

FOREWORD

I n this modern world of ours where science is integral to our everyday life, fantasy is sometimes forgotten and what is integral to fantasy is what *we* call magic. Magic like science can be beautiful or horrific. It can bring joy or it can bring desolation. It can help explain the things which normal logic cannot.

The magic of love is one such example and it can be beautiful or if twisted for selfish ends, becomes an abomination. Magic also plays on our senses and perception where in many instances is but an illusion.

Therein, I think, lies its horror where many a times we get lost in its manifold of truth and falsehoods. So telling a story is, I think, like weaving magic and therefore not easy but for the following story do read it in the light of the Russian Revolution. Then ponder upon it. For it was intended to be magical and it is at its core, still, just a story.

At the end of the day do you know the face behind the clown?

The tavern was a small but cozy place for the village locals to gather and relax. The building was built out of pinewood from the forests, with a bar counter for the owner to overlook the tavern grounds, which were littered with wooden tables and stools for its customers. In a small corner at the right side of the room was a fireplace that was currently burning bright during this autumn period.

Several villagers were already in the tavern early this evening. The full moon was out this night and its enchanting bright glow was illuminating the village on this cloudless autumn night. The strong smell of lamb stew, from a small kitchen at the back of the tavern, was filling the room mixing with the scented smell of the wood burning in the fireplace.

A circus troupe had just stopped, this afternoon, by the outskirts of the town. The tavern owner was expecting a crowd this night and had brought out kegs of freshly brewed ale. By the fireplace sat a burly young man, who was a wood-cutter, and an old man with tangled white hair and a face as wrinkled as the bark of a tree.

The wood-cutter then turned to the old man.

Wood-cutter - A fine night this is.

The old man replied in a bland voice.

Old man – Aye.

The wood-cutter continued, still smiling while taking a sip of his ale.

Wood-cutter – With the circus troupe here we might be able to watch a performance and catch up on some news.

Old man – As you say.

Sighed the old man while staring blankly into the fireplace.

Seeing that the old man was not very keen on having a conversation the wood-cutter decided to keep to himself and began to scan the tavern floor. Most of the people around were from the village except for a few, who looked like travelers who had just arrived, as they still had their packs on them. Trying in vain to find someone from the circus, he realized that they were probably still setting up camp or having their supper.

The old man suddenly turned to face the wood-cutter.

Old man - Young man. What do you think of our village?

The wood-cutter jerked back to see the old man looking at him solemnly, after a moment's pause he replied.

Wood-cutter - I think it's good.

Old man – It's quiet isn't it.

The wood-cutter nodded.

The old man then stared back at the fireplace, seemingly thinking of something.

Old man – Young man. Have you heard of Yankikovich the clown?

The wood-cutter just shrugged and shook his head.

Looking solemnly into the fireplace again the old man then said.

Old Man – During the time of the Tzar we had a burgomaster. He lived in a stone house on a hill not far from here. I was about your age then, probably slightly older, and I was a wood-cutter too.

The wood-cutter then leaned forward so as to be able to hear more clearly as the old man continued with his story.

*****

[Old man's story]

A circus troupe once came into town. In it were the usual performers that every circus troupe would have. However this troupe was different. It had Yankikovich. One would suppose, that was not his real name but then again who he really was, is not of any importance. *Yankikovich the Clown* was a name that had passed from the lips of many travelers who passed through the village. It was said that he was a clown of many talents, a unique sort of clown. He could perform various stunts, magic, sing and dance in his own clownish sort of way.

All who mentioned him said he brought joy and laughter to all his audiences. It was most probable that almost every circus ringleader would be glad to have him in their troupe. It was also said that he once performed for the Tzar and he so thoroughly enjoyed the performance that the Tzar decided to grant him a boon.

Yankikovich could have asked for anything. Land, wealth or even a hand in marriage for he was described to possess the looks of a charming enough young man when he presented himself formally before the Tzar. However he did not ask for these things, instead he told the Tzar that his greatest desire was to bring joy to everyone that he met. Thus if a boon be granted to him, he hoped that the Tzar would help spread the fame of his performance throughout the land so that he might travel freely to other parts to spread joy and laughter.

The Tzar being wise was surprised yet happy with the answer that Yankikovich gave him. Knowing this to be a good thing, since his role as a Tzar was to also bring happiness and prosperity to his land, the Tzar granted Yankikovich his boon and told all his subjects to mention Yankikovich where ever they might pass.

Word had, of course, passed to our village and so everyone was excited to have the circus troupe nearby.

The burgomaster was a rather fat man who had a wife and one daughter. He was an ostentatious man. He had grown fat from the land but he seldom troubled the villagers as long as we paid our dues. He also had a retinue of armed guards, which he claimed was sequestered from the Tzar himself but even with their striking uniforms we knew they were men under his employment. They could be hard when required and would sometimes, on their own, request for some payment in kind from the villagers for their rendered services.

Hearing the coming of the circus troupe the burgomaster decided to throw a feast and invited Yankikovich to perform at the feast. Yankikovich then agreed and attended the feast the following night.

*****

[At the feast]

The feast was an extravagant affair, which took the villagers a whole day to prepare. The tables were laid out, food, wine and ale had to be carried up and prepared. Come nightfall, almost everyone from the village and the troupe were at the large field just outside of the burgomaster's house. Large fire briers were lit up in large iron torch stands. When it was time for Yankikovich to perform he stood in the middle of the whole crowd in costume and with his props.

He entertained everyone with his tricks and stunts. The burgomaster could be visibly seen enjoying the whole performance. Then towards the end of his performance he requested for the burgomaster to participate in the coming act. The burgomaster agreed and was told to bring along his mug of ale. A request was then made for the mug to be fully filled and passed to Yankikovich. Yankikovich then drank from the mug and pretending to be drunk spilled some of the ale while complementing this must be the best ale he had ever drunk. Everyone laughed.

He then requested again for more ale. Then when trying to drink from the mug made a curious look at the mug, scratched his head and overturned the mug over his face. To everyone's surprise nothing came out of the recently filled mug. He then passed the mug back to the burgomaster and asked him to drink from it. After doing so the burgomaster also looked curiously at the mug and poured some ale out of the mug for all to see before looking up curiously at the crowd.

Subsequently a male villager was asked to step forward and Yankikovich extended out an empty palm upon which suddenly a yellow flame burst forth, afloat on his palm. Everyone suddenly stood transfixed upon the flame. The villager was asked to also extend out an empty palm for Yankikovich to pass the flame to him but the flame extinguished itself just as it touched the villager's hand.

Yankikovich then scratched his head and turned towards the burgomaster, now holding on to a full mug of ale. The burgomaster was then asked to then put down his mug and hold out two hands. Yankikovich reignited the flames again, now holding it carefully with his two hands, and attempted to pass it over to the burgomaster. The flames did not extinguish when placed on the burgomaster's hands. Murmurings of astonishment started to come up among the villagers. Even Yankikovich was staring at the burgomaster astonished.

The flame illuminated the burgomaster's face. His eyes were intently staring at the flame he now held in his hands. He then tried to hold it with one hand and was surprised that it did not fade away. Now amused at this development the burgomaster then juggled the flame over to his other hand and it remained burning. All eyes were now observing the burgomaster and the flame.

The burgomaster, probably feeling more confident, then started to juggle the flame between both hands. When suddenly! The flame exploded and set the burgomaster ablaze. Everyone panicked.

Yankikovich immediately reached forth for the burgomaster's mug on the floor to splash out the ale but nothing came out. He quickly passed it over to the villager he had called out and asked him to splash but even though he succeeded, the flames now covering the whole of the burgomaster's upper body, continued to burn.

Shouts of panic erupted and the crowd went wild. Luckily, a group of men thought quickly to uncap a whole keg of ale and poured it out upon the burgomaster. The flames died out. The burgomaster who was flailing about in panic, now stood drenched with ale and not a hair or cloth burnt by the flames.

Yankikovich then went over to the burgomaster to double check and threw up his hands with a smile, as if in triumph, and took several bows before a stunned audience. A few moments later, when we all realized it was all part of the trick, everyone present broke out in raucous laughter. Everyone except the burgomaster.

The burgomaster as if waking up from a daze, after being unceremoniously drenched, immediately signaled for his armed guards who were standing just behind his table. They swiftly poured in next to him and before the whole crowd could stop their laughter, Yankikovich was seized.

Yankikovich was then forced to leave the field with the guards and the whole feast came to a halt. Everyone was dismissed.

The next day the circus troupe left. Word got out from the burgomaster's servants that Yankikovich was killed. There were many accounts on how it happened. Some say he was beheaded, others say he was burnt alive and another version said he was tortured before dying. Reason given for punishment was misdemeanor. A wave of sadness came over the whole village that day.

The following day however, more news came from the servants. They said that the burgomaster had disappeared. The whole village went out to search for the burgomaster but to no avail. One of the old men from the village then went over to the burgomaster's house to provide condolence to the wife. But the tale he brought back later made all who heard it fall into a deep silence.

He reported that the wife had found the burgomaster missing from their bed the next morning. Thinking he might have gone off to another room to sleep she thought nothing of it before going off later to find him. Yet after going through every room she could not find him or anything signifying he was there. The strange thing was that when she got back to her room, she found the mug that he had during the feast resting on a small wooden table beside his side of the bed. And the mug was filled with ale that was warm which she mentioned was strange, as her husband does not drink warm ale. She had left it there as she went on to inquire with the servants but none of them had left it there and none would dare enter her room without her permission or request. Even stranger still was that after the completion of the search, the mug of ale she had left in her room was still warm and she even showed it to him, he swore.

The old man then paused upon completion of his tale. The wood-cutter looking attentively at him.

Old man – Until today I still do not know what happened. I have my suspicions but… (The old man shook his head.) I think only heaven knows what truly transpired. A new burgomaster was sent to us several months later and several months later we received news that the Tzar regime had toppled.

The wood-cutter then looked towards the yellow flames of the fireplace and pondered upon the tale which he had just heard.

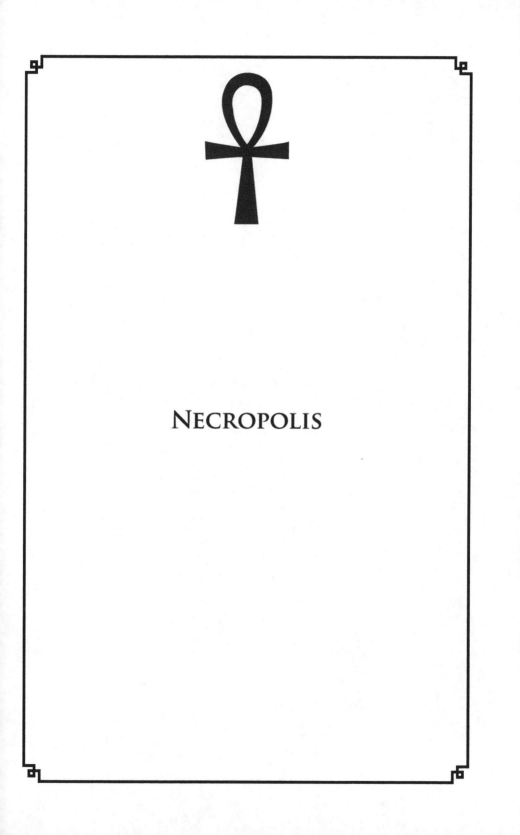

NECROPOLIS

FOREWORD

War is something that is considered deep for contemplation. Most would agree it is a rather dark topic for discussion. But yet it is the very thing which permeates the history of mankind.

War in itself is not wrong but it is the pretext of war which can make it deplorable and even horrific. However, given the right pretext, it would be honorable or even necessary to be a part of it.

Yet war itself, under any circumstance, is horrible with the violence it involves and its untold horrors. The seemingly benign qualities that make it so much more detestable, is many a times the silent drama that precedes it. Its silence gradually producing a complex web of black and white, weaving across each other like a spiders web and, ironically, like piano keys produce a million tunes all intertwining with each other. It is in the midst of this evolving chaos that results in war.

A chaos, that upon contemplation, can be just as depressing as the chaos which war itself produces. Ironically it is also in this chaos that lessons can perhaps be gleaned after contemplation. Lessons that can perhaps help us prevent another similar event or prevent us from being caught unaware.

Thus it is with this that I think we should respect the silent memorials erected to commemorate the wars that have passed. For without contemplation, I am afraid history is bound to repeat itself again.[1]

---

[1]   A suggestion is to listen to a song by Katie Melua titled "Spider's Web". Search on Youtube.

Listen to the sounds of silence.

If history repeats itself, and the unexpected always happens, how incapable must Man be of learning from experience. **George Bernard Shaw** *- Irish dramatist, socialist & a co-founder of the* <u>London School of Economics</u>

O siris was about to put the finishing touches to the pyramid before enclosing it with the final building block at its top. Isis was by his side ensuring that all that was required to be placed in the pyramid, to be sealed, was inside. Inside the pyramid, besides the sarcophagus of the Lord who died, were also many precious metals and gems which were either fashioned into various ornaments or had records of the Lord's heroic deeds inscribed upon them. Such was the scale and skill of the constructions that it could only be the work of gods.

Osiris then sighed, turned towards Isis and asked.

Osiris – What is it that corrupts a man's heart? What is it that makes a man's heart heavier than a Roc's feather such that he may not pass on to the afterlife? Are we mad to do this?

Isis – The riches that we bury here will be worth the Lord's sacrifice. He had after all been willing to sacrifice his all despite the odds during the Great War. And by doing what we do now, it would help preserve the peace we have earned for the many years to come.

Osiris – I think you are right.

Osiris nodded slowly in agreement. *The great riches which drove the Great War and corrupted the hearts of many men should indeed be buried. It is also fitting that it is through our burial of the dead, especially one of the War's heroes, that this deed is achieved. Their spirits would approve of this.*

Isis – My only fear is that man is prone to forget. Should one day man uncover this place and forget its sacredness, who knows what manner of a curse or blessing would be borne out of their discovery?

Osiris – That is why we have included writings in metal, which record the life of this man and the corruption he had fought against during the Great War.

Staring solemnly at the North Star, overhead, Osiris turned his gaze back upon the nearly finished pyramid. Osiris slowly proceeded to place the final block on top of the pyramid to seal it. This was followed by a sandstorm upon the abandoned desert which covered the completed pyramid built within a hollow dug out from the desert sands. Then left Osiris and Isis, leaving behind an empty landscape of sand and wind.

*****

[British archeological expedition in Egypt]

The campsite was buzzing with activity. They had just made an astounding archeological find. Several blocks of stones stacked on top each other, like a miniature pyramid, to a height of about two men could be seen poking out of the sandy ground. Men were now trying to find a way to properly remove the lone large block on the top of the block stack.

The top block of stone had been discovered about a week ago. They had at first thought nothing of it but it encouraged them to step up their efforts to excavate further. It was only when they had discovered it to be most likely part of a pyramid that everyone began to become more excited.

A slightly rotund man, wearing a straw hat with a pair of spectacles underneath and sporting a black beard was standing by the base of the pyramid structure, under the hot sun. He was an English Professor of Archeology, and was the director of the archeological site. He was gazing intently on the Egyptian workmen who were trying to remove the top stone block. He strongly believed that what they have found was the top of a buried pyramid and if they were able to uncap its top, whatever wonders were hidden within would be revealed to them.

This, in his mind, would probably be as astounding a discovery as the Rosetta Stone which was discovered by accident during Napoleon's battle for Egypt.

As he observed the workmen he realized that there was no easy way to remove the stone. It was too heavy and even if they tied ropes to pull it off it would be too dangerous for the workmen below when the stone comes tumbling down. The workmen have been at it the whole morning and it was now noon. In his anxious mind he was pondering that perhaps it was time to try something new.

He then called for the manager of the workmen.

Professor – We have dynamite. I think we can use that to blow the block up while we stand a safe distance away.

Manager – But is this right? If we are truly standing on a pyramid then this is sacred ground. I fear offending the gods and the spirits.

Professor – I think you do not need to worry about that. From where I come from we believe that there is only one God that rules over all. He is the God who brought Moses out of Egypt. Something which neither RA nor Osiris could stop.

The professor spoke confidently.

The manager just nodded and proceeded to call the workmen down from the pyramid to give them their new orders.

[Block has been blown apart]

After surrounding the stone block with dynamite and blowing it up, they now waited for the debris to settle. The professor had already readied by his side a portable oil lamp and a very long bundle of rope. He then spoke to the manager, informing him of his plan to tie a rope around himself so that he might be lowered slowly down through the hole at the top.

Once the debris had settled the professor immediately put his plan into action. The manager then arranged for five men to assist in the descent. The men would be holding the rope to control the professor's descent down the hole where four men would act as anchors for the rope while the fifth who was nearest to the professor would slowly feed in more rope to lower the professor down the hole.

The professor now stood dangerously upon the edge of the pyramid's opening. He gradually placed himself into a sitting position on the opening's ledge. He then turned his head to face the workmen holding onto the rope to see if they were ready and holding firmly onto the rope. When he was satisfied, he then slowly lowered himself into the hole and let himself hang freely from the rope tied around him. The manager then passed him a lit oil lamp, which the professor held tightly with his right hand.

The professor then nodded to the manager, to give the signal, for the men to lower him.

Down the dark hole he went, with the little illumination he had from the little oil lamp of his. As he slowly dropped lower into the dark emptiness around him, sometimes jerking precariously, he tried as best as he could to pierce the darkness with the light from his lamp. But the descent was only filled with darkness.

Scary it might be but the excitement of a new discovery goaded him to push on and not give up. He patiently, yet anxiously, awaited for his feet to hit ground.

After what seemed almost like an eternity, his feet finally felt something. As he was lowered some more he was then able to plant his feet firmly on whatever he was standing on. His rope also started to slacken thus allowing him to move around slightly. He lowered his lamp to view what laid underneath his feet and to his surprise, when the light of his lamp fell upon the "ground" it seemed to glitter. Amazed he bent down further to have a closer look.

What he saw glittering back at him was as astounding as the darkness that surrounds him. For he thought to himself, *is this gold?*

*****

[Several months later back in England]

Several months have passed since the professor's discovery. About a week after his startling discovery he had quickly packed his things in preparation for a journey back to England. He had to immediately contact the museum's curator and personally make arrangements for the transportation and storage of the archeological finds.

It was currently afternoon in England and he had been invited to the curator's office for tea. He now sat in that very office which was rather large and filled with cabinets holding files on the museum's pieces. Together with the curator they were seated by a small tea table situated next to a window overlooking a wide courtyard. The bright sunlight was shining upon them as the curator's secretary was serving them their tea.

The curator waited for the secretary to leave before starting their discussion proper.

Curator – I believe you are here with regard to the letter you sent me several months back while you were still in Egypt?

The curator placed two cubes of sugar into his tea.

The professor also calmly followed suite and replied.

Prof – Yes. Quite so. Might I enquire if there are any storehouses for the storage of our archeological find?

Curator – Yes there are. But what exactly did you find? You failed to elaborate much in your letter except to say it was the discovery of the century. Almost equaling the discovery of the Rosetta Stone.

The curator stirred his tea cup as he looked at the professor curiously.

Prof – My apologies. You must understand that I was quite excited by my find and was very anxious to get back to make the proper arrangements.

Curator – It is quite all right. No need to apologize. I understand. Please continue.

Prof – What I have found is something which could change the world. It is hard to explain in full what I have discovered as even I myself have not fully understood it. But in summary, what I have found is a treasure trove of ancient Egyptian artifacts. All made of precious metals and gems, which blasphemous it might be for me to say, might even rival the riches of Solomon's Temple. However, this is not even its truest value, as on these artifacts are inscribed what I believe to be the recorded history of the sarcophagus.

The sarcophagus I found was caste in gold and was surprisingly large. There were also large metallic steles with ancient hieroglyphics engraved on them. It truly is a challenge to describe to you what I have seen.

Even now as we speak the people I have at the camp site are probably still figuring out how to excavate and move the artifacts discovered.

The professor paused and looked at the curator intently. The curator was now pondering seriously over what the professor had said.

Curator – How many of these artifacts are there actually?

Prof – If my estimates are not wrong the dark cavern is about the ground size of Kensington Park. Not to mention many of these artifacts were piled on top of each other.

The curator looking surprised then exclaimed.

Curator - That would require a damn whole lot of storehouse space!

The professor nodded in return.

Curator – Looks like we are going to need the expertise of the Company. Only they would have the resources to handle the enormity of your find and they would also have the storehouses you require. I believe we should be able to convince them to be a part of this great endeavor.

Prof – Yes, I think you are right. With their extensive trade routes and business contacts they would definitely be most suited for the job.

Both of them smiled and raising their teacups proposed a toast to each other.

*****

The door to the museum curator's office suddenly burst opened. The curator shocked, quickly looked up from behind his desk, which was just opposite the double doors, and found the archeological professor striding rapidly towards his desk.

The professor slammed both his palms upon the front of the curator's desk, while still panting heavily from his evident rush to the office.

Prof – My dear friend. I have very bad news. The camp site has been ravaged! Apparently by bandits.

The curator raised his left eyebrow and looked at the professor in disbelief.

Prof – We have lost everything. The bandits took everything after killing everyone at the camp site.

When the words of the professor finally sunk in the curator exclaimed.

Curator - My dear Lord! How can this be. It has already been about three months since we last spoke. All preparations are already on the way for the Company to take over security and transportation of the artifacts.

They stared at each other for a moment.

Prof - We need to conduct an investigation into this matter! Technically those items are now under the ownership of the Company. I am sure they will not let this incident simply pass them by.

Curator – This seems to be the only way forward.

Prof – All that we have done has gone down the drain!

The professor slammed his hands angrily against the table.

*****

[A business meeting in Egypt]

The German businessman was seated on a carpet of elaborate design within the confines of a large Bedouin tent. He was in Egypt searching out for new business ventures. Glass ware and carpets being one of the few trade items being considered. He had been informed of this lucrative business deal through his contacts.

He had been waiting in the sparsely decorated tent for almost half an hour. During the wait he had been wondering why his Egyptian contact had told him that *This was a business deal that the gods have given to you.* From his own personal experience, rarely do Egyptians make such references, especially in front of a foreigner.

And even though he was a staunch modernist, believing that gods or spirits do not create the reality we live in but logic and the choices man makes, his contact's statement did pique his interest.

There was a sudden rustle in the tent's flap behind him just before it was flung opened. Three men entered. The man in the centre was of medium built and wore just a simple tunic and pants with a scarf wrapped around his neck, while the two men by the side were burly and bare bodied with a scarf wrapped around their necks.

The men calmly walked in and once opposite him, the centre man sat on the carpet while the other two stood beside him with their arms folded.

Egyptian – Greetings. I am sorry for having made you wait for so long.

German – Apology accepted. I am not offended. You have a very nice carpet laid out and the tent is cool.

Replied the German fluently, in the Bedouin dialect.

The Egyptian then smiled.

Egyptian - I see that you speak our language. I am pleasantly surprised.

The German bowed slightly in return.

Egyptian – I believe you have been informed of the business proposal which I have for you?

German – Yes, I have been informed. But what exactly are you intending to trade? Carpets?

The Egyptian laughed.

Egyptian - No. What I have is far more valuable to you than mere carpets.

The Egyptian then clapped his hands twice and a man servant walked into the tent carrying in his hands one of the largest diamonds which the German has ever set eyes on. The size of the diamond was about the size of his head.

As the German stared at the diamond, the Egyptian spoke.

Egyptian - This is what I have to trade and I have much more. Including gold, silver and other precious metals and stones that you have not set your eyes on.

The German then composed himself.

German - What would you desire in return for the trade?

Egyptian – I would require food, amenities and weapons.

The German looked solemnly at the diamond which had been placed in front of him. *This is indeed an enticing deal. Such precious stones and metals would be worth a large sum of money in Europe.*

German – You have any of the precious metals to show me?

The Egyptian then clapped his hands and another man servant walked in carrying a large block of solid gold which had the length, breath and height of an average Egyptian square cushion. Now he was really intrigued.

German – Where did you find such riches?

Egyptian – We came across a hidden cavern and found them. It took us great pains to transport them across the desert. They are now safely hidden at a safe location. If you wish to make the trade we will make arrangements for the treasures to be transported to your ships.

The German did not fully believe the Egyptian's account, but given the privilege that he has been given to be the sole proprietor of this trade, this would be a small risk in comparison to the great rewards which he and his partners would reap.

Without further consideration the German promptly replied.

German - Yes. I will make the trade. But first I would need to at least inspect these treasures which you have acquired and then speak to my partners before providing you anymore details.

Egyptian – Of course. However we would need to blindfold you before taking you to inspect the treasures. I hope you understand.

The German nodded.

German – I do. For the treasure's safety. When do we depart?

Egyptian – Tonight. The journey would be cooler.

*****

The morning sun was shining bright as a cool wind blowed across the field. The professor was strolling across the field in Kensington Garden towards the museum curator who was already standing below a tree waiting for him.

The curator waved at the professor.

Curator - Good Morning.

The professor waved back as he strolled faster towards the curator.

Prof – Sorry for keeping you waiting.

Curator – That's alright. The Company has apprised me on the progress of their investigations and thought that you would probably want to know.

Prof – I was thinking that was why you called for this meeting.

Curator – Shall we take a stroll?

Prof – Yes. Let's do.

Both men proceeded to walk across the lush field in the bright morning sun.

Curator – The world is a large place. Even with steam boats it still takes a while to travel across distances. Thus with several months already passed since our last meeting the Company has not been able to make much progress on what has happened to the treasures. They have managed to check on what was left of the camp site but they were not able to find any significant clues.

The curator sighed.

Curator – I am afraid more time is needed for the investigations before anything conclusive can be arrived at.

Prof – I have also made checks of my own with my contacts and nothing significant seemed to have popped up. Except that a lucrative business deal had been closed in Egypt.

Curator – Hmm… That might be worth checking out some more. But I think the bandits would have most probably broken down the artifacts into smaller pieces for sale.

Prof – I guess it was all just a stroke of really bad luck then.

The professor depressingly shrugged.

Curator – Not to worry. I am sure that there are more archeological mysteries to be discovered. I hear there are new archeological digs being performed in Egypt or you could try ancient Mesopotamia which is further down south in Africa.

Prof – Think I had better consider involving the Company the next time. They would be able to provide security for the site and also transportation should there be any finds.

They continued strolling, now towards the museum. Both wondering what really happened and considering if there were any other ways to help in the investigation.

*****

After a long journey across the desert on a camel's back they finally stopped. The German was carefully helped off the camel and was then led away by one of the servants. As he walked blindfolded he soon entered an area where a cool draft could be felt blowing across his face. He then felt the heat of a torch being lighted up beside him before he was led further towards the cool draft. They continued walking for about half an hour before finally stopping.

His blindfold was then taken off and as his eyes began to accustom themselves to the sudden brightness from the torches he realized that he was in a cavern. As his vision grew clearer, he gazed to the front and was surprised to see heaps of gem stones and precious metals all placed neatly before him. Smooth solid blocks of various metals and large gemstones glimmered under the light of the numerous flickering torches.

Where did they ever find such riches? This is truly the treasure of treasures!

The massiveness of the cavern hinted to him just how much there were being stored here.

The income that can be generated from selling all this treasure in Europe or Russia could possibly remake Germany's standing and presence in the world!

Then the burning question of where they had found such riches crept up into his mind.

German – This is truly a magnificent sight. But I am afraid I have to ask. Where did you *truly* find all these?

The Egyptian paused to consider the query. Then solemnly answered.

Egyptian – We found these in caverns like this. Apparently there are many buried under the sands and it was our blessing to have found it.

The German paused. "But why trade it with us when you can sell it away yourselves?"

Egyptian – Our people have no need of such treasures. What we need is food, clothing and a safe place to live. And since we have no one to sell to around Egypt or with our neighbours we would sell it to your people instead. I am quite sure these things are worth far more in your country then ours.

The German shocked beyond words just nodded in return.

Egyptian – So are you still willing to proceed with the trade?

The German still recovering from his shock took some time to consider his reply.

German – Yes... We will. I will also assure you that I will personally ensure that your people get the food and whatever else they should need. What you have given to us can provide for your people for several generations.

The Egyptian smiled.

Egyptian - I thank you for your offer.

With that the German and Egyptian shook each other's hands firmly before the blindfold was placed back upon the German again. Then as they made their way out of the cavern the German was beginning to ponder within his mind -- how this glorious find can one day make Germany *truly glorious*.

*****

[After World War I]

A lonely young man stood in a cemetery in Munich. The area was allocated for many of the dead soldiers of the First World War. He stood solemnly staring at the tombstone of one of the fallen. In his mind he was wondering *why did they have to surrender?*

He recalled the times when they joked in the bunk protected by tons of steel from the sea water surrounding their U-boat. They had felt invincible being undetectable and being able to outrun any ship. They often questioned themselves but in the end were quite sure that they were not merciless killers. They left their enemy's life boats alone and if possible would try to radio out for a ship to rescue them. In their mind they were just trying to fight a fair war which was probably the best kind of war that could be fought.

The grave he stood in front of was one of his childhood friends who had been conscripted into the infantry and had died mid-way in the war. Many had died in the war, perhaps more than any other war. The heavy burden that all Germans now have to carry after the Treaty of Versailles, weighs heavily upon him, probably more so than any other German. For he holds the burden of his father.

The man's father had been a businessman. He had been blessed with a very lucrative trade in Egypt. Through the trade he had become rich and being a loyal German, much of his money had been invested in the strengthening of Germany that included the building of roads, ports and even maintaining a weapons factory.

His father had sent him to one of the renown Universities of Germany. He had chosen to study Engineering but he also had an interest in other subjects like literature and philosophy. Being part of the higher strata of Germany also allowed him to understand that in relation to other parts of Europe Germany was much ahead in terms of modern thought, science and technology. All thanks to their dear "Old Fritz".

He smiled at the thought of "Old Fritz" as he continued to look upon the grave stone. His father was also a learned man of vision like "Old Fritz" who respected all cultures. He had often shared with him his dreams and he was aware that unlike the other European countries Germany was not a very *colonialistic* country. Therefore in the world stage it only had its industry, sciences and most importantly its people to propel it forward in the face of stiff European competition. The trade his father had acquired in Egypt had been the Holy Grail for Germany's development and developed it did, at an industrious pace.

Yet in one fell swoop the dreams of Germany were shattered. Its political leaders had signed Germany away in the midst of the War. Even though Germany was leading at the War front, they had decided without consulting Germany's citizens, that Germany had to surrender. The reason given being that the war had been drawn out long enough and that Germany was at fault even when it all started because Germany had been affronted by the sudden assassination of the Archduke of Austria.

What however saddens the young German most, was that the day after the signing over of Germany to the Allied powers he was out at sea, when his father died, supposedly of a heart attack.

Before dying his father had left him a sealed letter that was addressed only to him.

Dear Son,

Ever since your mother died you were the apple of my eye. I have always sought the best for you just as I sought out the best for Germany. I now write this with great regret that the fall of Germany, which you would soon hear of, is partially related to me. I have not much time as the investigators would soon be upon me to carry me off for questioning. So in short, it all has to do with what happened in Egypt. The Treasure which I found was originally supposed to be under British possession. According to the first visit by the investigators.

Enclosed within the letter are details with regard to the bank accounts which I have. Please help me to take care of them and await my return. The British investigators might be bringing me over to Britain for questioning so the situation would take some time to settle. Take care of yourself.

Love,
Father

It was with these burdens in his heart which he now moves through life. Including this internal struggle within him of being the scion of a large inheritance, although now diminished somewhat by the Treaty of Versailles and the British investigators and having to face up to the brewing hatred he has within him for the oppression which Germany now has to go through because of its politicians. The country of Germany was now to him nothing but a nation of the dead. *Who would understand my struggles and my pain?*

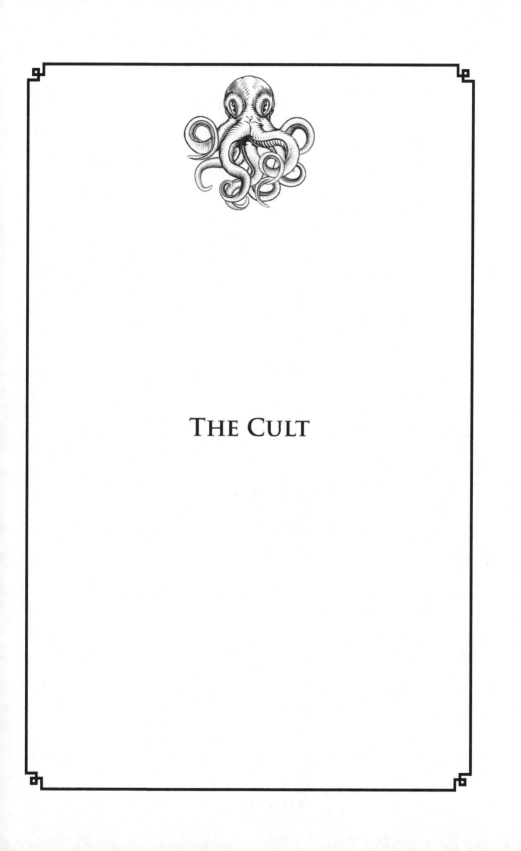

THE CULT

FOREWORD

What is horror? I think horror has to be alien and anything alien can be horrific. That, I think, is horror.

However, sometimes true horror can be hard to identify. For it has embedded itself, in our quaint little world, as something which is natural. Such that the phrase "how dark is the darkness when darkness is light" becomes all so poignant.

Beware the horrors of this world for they do exist, albeit hidden.

The room was illuminated only by the street light outside as the room lights were not turned on. There was the shuffling of feet and the rustling of clothes as Jim emptied his cupboard. He was trying to pack as much as he could into a large traveling suitcase. He had a mini mag-light in his right hand to assist him when he was unable to find his way about in the darkness, although he would always make sure that he did not shine the torch directly onto the window curtains.

He had just rushed back after a late night at the office. He had been "working" late into the night. His office was on the thirty-eighth floor of the sixty floor high building. The top floors of the building were where the magnificent views of the city could be seen and it was also where the magnificently powerful reside. And where they reside is where rumors reside, as well, for anyone one who has the ears to tune in to the right frequency.

He had it all planned out. He had managed to get the keys from security, for one night, for a favor and tonight was going to be the night that he gets the scoop of a lifetime. The plan was simple, wait till everyone had left then make his move. However nothing could prepare him for what he saw at the very top floor.

For when he had made his way up, climbing the flight of stairs all the way up as elevator access was controlled at night, he crept down the corridors of the top-most floor and came upon a large packed auditorium. The lights were dimmed and he had stood by what seemed to be the top right entrance to the auditorium and was met by a strange sight on the stage down below.

Standing, under a spotlight on the stage, behind what looked like a golden book stand was a figure in a dark colored suit and a bright colored tie. He seemed to be reading from the large hardcover book placed on the book stand. The words uttered were however foreign and incomprehensible to Jim. Yet they were strangely alluring and hypnotic as his mind was drawn to the words uttered. Soon everyone else seated in the aisle were also uttering the same words and he was nearly tempted to utter the words out loud but with some effort of will, he managed to keep himself from doing so.

After forcing himself out of the trance, he then forced himself to focus on the stage. Then for some inexplicable reason, as if his eyes were playing tricks on him, he noticed that a dark shadow seemed to coalesce behind the speaker. As he focused harder upon this strange phenomenon, he noticed what seemed to be two orbs of red light fading to life. This confused him slightly but as he tried to make sense of what he was witnessing he began to feel that the orbs looked like eyes and the nebulous shadow coalescing seems to be a face of sorts.

Suddenly the chanting slowly faded away and his mind started to feel heavy and he began to feel a foreboding presence hovering behind. Yet when he looked behind there was nothing. When he turned back to look at the stage the red orbs now seemed to be staring back at him. Just then, words began to coalesce within his mind. *Jim… Jim… Is here.*

Immediately after those words appeared in his mind the speaker looked towards his direction staring at him. Now as Jim now had a better look at the speaker's face he noticed that he was a balding old man with a wrinkly face. A quick estimate was that the speaker was probably about seventy years of age.

The speaker's hand then lifted and pointed towards his direction. *Jim must die! He now knows.*

Surprised at the words which formed in his mind and the sudden turn in events, he immediately headed for the staircase landing. Upon entering, he quickly locked the door to the landing and ran all the way down, as fast as he could, to the fortieth floor where he knew that at least one elevator would be stationed during the night.

He had then, by some stroke of luck, managed to make his way to his SUV in the underground carpark and sped all the way back home.

*****

[After packing]

He stood for a moment wondering if there was anything else he might have forgotten. Then placing the passport he held in his right hand into his jacket pocket he pulled his suitcase out the backdoor. After locking the backdoor he made his way towards the garage. He then placed the suitcase onto the back seat of his SUV before moving on to the driver's seat.

He placed his traveling back pack onto the passenger seat and seated himself calmly in the driver's seat. Recollecting all that he had learnt during his two years working in the corporation, he now had to decide on a new course of action. This new turn of events was beginning to overturn everything he had known.

Firstly, he knew he needed to get away. Secondly, he needed to relook at everything he knew and get the information out. But how he was suppose to achieve all these without getting caught was the challenge he now faced.

Seated in his SUV, in the darkness of his garage, he finally decided that the first thing he had to do was to get away to some where safe. A place he could be alone and anonymous. He had more than sufficient savings to subsist for several years without a job. So at that very moment he started his engine, turned off his mobile phone and drove out onto the drive way with the Airport being the destination in mind.

*****

[Thinking while driving along towards the airport]

As Jim drove he began to reflect on what he had just experienced.

Apparently what he had seen was not normal. Actually whatever "rumors" he had managed to dig up this past two years had not been normal. The whole corporation had been a global force to be reckoned with.

He had joined as an executive managing the manpower matters of the corporation. He specifically dealt with finances, meaning he helped made sure that employees get the fair share of their salaries. So more or less he was placed at a very central location within the corporation and was privy to much of the office gossip going around.

He knew that the corporation was big but he never expected it to have such great clout, with its tendrils embedded across different parts of the globe. It had investments and deep connections within other companies and corporations which allow it to manipulate the world stage. It was so extensive that it even had connections with government agencies and this was another good reason why he had to get away soon.

But what he had witnessed this night was something of an anomaly which baffled and terrified him. The alien presence that had spoken within his mind had left a foreboding feeling within him. Even now he still felt as if the presence was still with him and that it had just decided to keep silent. This whole episode was like something out of a scary Sci-fi movie.

He was quite sure that he was not under the influence of any drug or fumes as his mind felt normal throughout the whole experience, except when he had seen the two orbs of red light and heard the voice in his head.

He was quite sure that whatever the entity that spoke in his mind *it* would surely accomplish the task. For the urgency and insistence in the voice was unmistakable. It would be surmised to believe that everyone else in the auditorium also heard it in their minds, if not, the speaker surely did. The simple logical outcropping from this event would simply mean that the corporation's tendrils would be crawling to seek him out very soon.

*****

[Upon reaching the airport]

After driving for a while in search of parking space he finally found one in the airport's open air car park. He then took out his luggage, locked his SUV and nonchalantly strolled towards the airport entrance. Upon reaching the entrance he was greeted by an airport staff who happened to be standing by the automatic twin sliding doors. The staff seemed to knowingly nod at him before continuing on her way.

Jim's eyes suddenly twitched. He did not know her. Yet she seemed to know him.

A spasm of fear then surged up within him. He then looked cautiously around and suddenly felt as if many eyes were eyeing him in passing. Even the covered surveillance camera seemed to be focusing at the entrance when he briefly looked at it, as he thought that he had caught a glimpse of the camera lens, under the bright lightings, through the very slightly translucent black spherical cover.

He fought against the paranoia that was about to grip him and made his way to the airline counter to purchase an air ticket for Amsterdam. After purchasing the ticket he made his way to the transit area to wait for his flight and also hoped for a little more privacy.

However, he was still unable to shrug off the feeling that eyes were watching him.

*****

The corporation is a multinational company. Its investments run from rice fields, scientific laboratories, tele-communications; basically anything that can turn a profit you can be sure it would be there. This includes government contracts. From the private commercial to the public space its tendrils extends almost everywhere. Almost every corner of this earth, including the North pole, can be connected to the corporation.

Like all things natural it would of course have competitors. Other corporations with competing investments in this small world of mankind. Together they wage a commercial war against each other, each trying to gain a larger portion of the commercial pie that the world has to offer. Such is their involvement in the global monetary cycle that they are what one would call predators while the smaller businesses become akin to prey.

Generally a symbiotic relationship exists between them, since under any circumstance, the predator cannot eat up all its prey lest its food source in the commercial chain dries up. There are, of course, benign corporations but the one he work's for is definitely not one of those.

However working for the corporation has definitely opened up his eyes. If one thinks that all the random happenings in the world, that gets reported in the news, are all disconnected; one would be surprised at the numerous coincidences, where like a flutter of a butterfly's wings these random incidences are able to spark off a tumble of effects that eventually connect to one singular outcome that the corporation desires.

Like it or not, in this globalised world *everything* can be somehow connected, especially when you know the rumors.

*****

In a small hotel, in Amsterdam, Jim was just filling in the finishing touches to his journal. A finished plate of scrambled eggs and toast rested just beside him. This is the third hotel he had been staying in, under a different name, for the past one week plus since he reached.

All this while, he had been feverishly writing, seeking to record down all that he had learnt regarding the corporation and its practices. He still had not worked out who he was going to pass this information to but later in the morning he was going to meet a contact who might actually know a suitable candidate.

Once he had finished writing he looked at the clock on his desk and was surprised that it was already ten o'clock. His contact was probably waiting at the hotel lobby by now. He quickly tidied up and holding his journal in his hand made his way down to the hotel lobby.

At the hotel lobby, he looked around for his contact. He saw him emerge from the rest room corridor by the corner. He smiled and went forward to shake his hand. His contact smiled back but for some reason Jim felt something out of place in the smile and when their hands touched, a familiar heavy feeling overtook his mind.

Jim. I have found you.

Then almost suddenly, Jim lost consciousness.

*****

[Back in the office]

It was a Monday afternoon. Jim had just got back from lunch with some colleagues. He had just gotten back from his trip in Amsterdam and he had been sharing with them the trip's experiences over lunch. He had never felt so refreshed. The decision to take the last minute holiday was probably one of the best decisions which he had ever made.

He had even met up with a good friend in Amsterdam and shared with him all the cares and woes about his work with the corporation.

A lady then walked up to him saying that he was wanted in the sixtieth floor. Jim was taken aback by the news. *The big boss wants to see me?* He quickly made his way to the elevator.

When the elevator opened at the sixtieth floor, it was Jim's first time there. Although for some strange reason the layout seemed familiar but Jim just shrugged it away. He then made his way down a corridor and found himself in front of two large glass doors. He then swung one open and walked to the secretary's desk just in front of him.

He then stated his name and the reason for being there. The secretary then replied in a sweet voice.

"Oh. It's you! The CEO is waiting for you inside. Please enter!"

Jim then entered into the CEO's office and saw a man in a dark suit with a bright colored tie sitting behind a large desk. The CEO looked up and smiled.

"Jim! I have been expecting you! Just the man that I wanted to see."

Jim walked over and the CEO stood up to shake Jim's hand. Jim then seated himself.

The CEO then looked at Jim intently.

"Jim. Have you read the news lately? There is a new wave coming upon the world. It is the new wave of global awareness on the duty of corporations, in the world, having a huge part to play in making our world a better place."

Jim vaguely remembered reading something like that. He nodded.

"The company would like you to lead a new project. We need someone who knows the company inside out. Someone who knows what the company has been doing wrong and who would like to see it corrected."

"I intend to give this opportunity to you, Jim! Would you agree to accept it?"

Jim was surprised a second time today. He did not know how to react. He just stared seriously at the CEO, as if in deep thought.

Then with a quick snap decision, "Yes! I would gladly accept your offer, Sir!"

"Very well then! I gladly refer you to the newly set up department on the fifty-eighth floor and you will be briefed upon your arrival. I am sure everyone there would be glad to see you!"

The CEO then stood up, firmly congratulating Jim on his new appointment before seeing him to the door.

Jim then walked out and slowly made his way down the corridor to the elevators. As he stood waiting for the elevator to take him to the fifty-eighth floor, the bright afternoon sun shined in through the windows like a new dawn.

THE JERUSALEM PARADOX

Foreword

*F*oundation of Harmony. What are the ingredients that form such a foundation? Two basic ingredients do come to mind. They are love and forgiveness. Love bind people together while forgiveness allows us to move on if we do make mistakes.

However in our conflict ridden world would these ingredients be sufficient? Would they be enough to bring us salvation?

[Inside a carpet shop somewhere in Jerusalem.]

The bell hanging upon the door rings as the door opens. Entering the shop is a bespectacled, semi-bald man with a well-trimmed moustache. The shop owner, a dark skin man with a bushy moustache, looks up while holding on to a broom.

It was around mid-afternoon, sunlight blazing through the shop's glass panels fell upon the carpets laid out in the shop front, keeping them warm.

Yesus - Good afternoon Ahmed. How goes your business?

Ahmed - As usual. It provides for me. Including the tea we are going to have later.

Ahmed smiles warmly.

Yesus - Aye.

Yesus makes a cursory look around the shop then walks towards a carpet clipped along the wall. Flipping up the shades clipped to his spectacles before reaching out to feel the carpet.

Yesus - I see that your carpets are getting finer. Looks like the hands that make them have not lost their touch. Good to know that there are still people who appreciate good carpets.

Ahmed - Indeed.

Ahmed finishes sweeping the last bit of dust into the dustpan.

Ahmed - Come. Let us go to the back for our tea. Help me lock the door and meet me in the kitchen.

Ahmed goes off to the back of the shop and empties his dustpan. He then sets aside the broom and dustpan before making his way to the cabinet for the teapot, cups, saucers and spoons. He places them onto a metal tray and brings them to a small round table in the middle of the kitchen. Yesus then enters the kitchen and walks towards the round table.

Ahmed - Help me arrange the cups on the table while I go prepare the water.

Ahmed proceeds to retrieve a metal kettle and after filling it with water, places it on an electrical induction stove. He then takes hold of a porcelain jar containing sugar cubes together with two teabags and walks back to the round table where Yesus is already seated with the metal tray placed on the floor beside him.

Yesus - Ah. No cakes and sweets?

Ahmed - Sorry my friend. I forgot about them.

Ahmed places the jar on the table and the teabags into the teapot. Then walks back to the cabinets where placed on the counter is a plate of cakes and Turkish sweets, covered by a dome plastic cover. Removing the cover he picks up the plate with both hands and proceeds back to the table again.

Ahmed - How goes life for you?

Yesus - All the same. Currently teaching Kantian philosophy. He is a hard one to understand.

Yesus gives a slight chuckle.

Yesus - German too.

Ahmed - Ah. Learning from the Germans. That is hard.

Smirking, Ahmed then places the plate down on the table and takes a sit on a white plastic chair, resting his back on the chair's back rest.

Ahmed - Shall we have a smoke while waiting for the water to boil?

Yesus - Sure. Why not.

Ahmed proceeds to light the sheesha standing beside the table. After several test puffs he passes the sheesha pipe to Yesus.

Yesus - Nothing like a good smoke to relieve the senses. Glad to know that you are taking good care of the sheesha I gave you.

Yesus takes a puff before blowing puffs of smoke into the air.

Ahmed - So what troubles you these days?

Yesus sighs.

Yesus - Many things. Like the recent retaliation against the rockets fired at us.

Ahmed - Yes. I heard a broadcasting station got "smart" bombed. Less television and radio for them now, eh...

Ahmed shakes his head while making a slight smirk.

Yesus - It is really a bad joke. Such an immense retaliation against their meagre rocket attacks. The rockets were not even "smart", most probably home-made. Thankfully none of our own people got hurt, which makes me beg the question of why such a violent retaliation.

Ahmed - Your people are a complicated people. But as you already know, every action calls for a reaction and when someone of higher authority gives an order the people below have to follow.

Yesus passes the pipe back to Ahmed.

Yesus - Yes. Our history is indeed complicated. The very day this land was ours it was already complicated. As sons Abraham, from the line of Isaac, we supposedly have rightful possession over this land. But our ancestors lost their right to the land when they disobeyed God as recorded in the Books Isaiah and Jeremiah. And even as they sought to regain it they lost it again for the same reason as recorded in Malachi.

Ahmed places the pipe in his mouth and takes a puff.

Yesus - Subsequently, the land was shared with people from other nations till the Roman Empire. With the Jewish Temple being the one unifying factor that gives us a sense of ownership over Jerusalem from the very beginning till AD 70.

Ahmed - Ah yes. AD 70. A very pivotal event with respect to the Temple. Some say it is the fault of the Roman empire under a paranoid Caesar who linked it to the rise in Christianity during that period. A minority think it is a result of Sadducee's politicking in Rome coupled with the rise in rebellious sentiments incited by the Pharisees in Jerusalem. Which I think is linked to my first point. But at the end of the day it shows God's disapproval of the Temple, does not matter whether you are Jewish or Christian. No miracle saved it.

The right side of Yesus lips rised slightly, seemingly in a smirk.

Ahmed - However, your people's current possession of the land is somewhat seen as a miracle and that troubles you?

Yesus - Yes. It is the foundation of what makes the situation so complicated. It has very far-reaching consequences existentially. But this is only one factor, the politicking which resulted in the formation of neo-Jerusalem and its continuation is also another problem which gives me migraines.

Ahmed - It is also the main reason why you are Atheistic?

Yesus nods back solemnly.

Ahmed - My people were mainly slaves during the Roman Empire. We have also shared this land with your people then. Even when Mohammad came and brought the rise in Islam and we became the new owners of the land we still shared it with others, including your people. We also faced the Western invaders together during the time of the Crusades. Our people have a shared history. Your dream of peace between our people is understandable.

Yesus - Sadly, reality is no dream.

Ahmed passes the pipe to Yesus apologetically and sighs.

Ahmed - Dreams are still what gives us hope my friend. It is what keeps us going.

Yesus - That is precisely the problem. What if the dream that gives us hope forces us into a maze of problems which we cannot navigate out of. My people, when they entered neo-Jerusalem after World War 2, just wanted a land of our own where we could live in peace and harmony. The principle was simple.

A frustrated frown appears on Yesus's face.

Ahmed - Then politics came into the picture and hands were forced into action culminating in the "miraculous" Seven Day War, where in order to protect your country's sovereignty, armed retaliation was unavoidable. For if your people were to lose the war, they would be lost and nationless, wanderers in the desert. Suffering the very same fate which my people in the Gaza now suffer.

Yesus smiles.

Yesus - How very sweet and understanding of you. Considering that my country owns the infrastructure in the Gaza.

Suddenly a whistling sound can be heard coming from the kettle. Ahmed rises to make his way to the kettle. Then carrying the kettle he walks to the table to pour the boiling water into the teapot before settling the kettle onto the floor beside the sheesha.

Yesus - This is where it gets existentialistic for me.

Ahmed - How so?

Yesus - You know me. I think a lot. So what I do not understand is the contradiction which this conflict has brought about for Christianity.

Ahmed - What about Judaism?

Yesus - That is a minor issue. The real thorn is a result of ultra-nationalistic sentiments within the establishment, which due to initial Western support for our country, has links to the "Christian" elements in the West.

I for one am a peace-activist. An atheist I may be but the precept of loving your neighbour is one I can understand. The teachings that Christ taught in the Beatitudes are good things. Being legalistic like the ultra-orthodox Jews is not going to make things any better.

However, if the Christians are in some way right, and believing in Christ is the only way to God and His heavenly Kingdom then in reality we have come to what is a major faux pas. No monotheistic religion seems right.

Ahmed - Indeed. The treatment that the people in the Gaza receive does not make things any better, does it. This makes both Judaism and Christianity look bad. Islam is also not placed in a very good light with the complicated political structure between the Middle-Eastern countries. Egypt and Saudi States being close "allies" while Iran and Syria stand in solidarity with the Palestinians.

When you look at it altogether, the contradictions surface and it looks like all of us might be heading for hell. Except maybe the Atheists if there really is no God.

Ahmed chuckles slightly. Then proceeds to lift his teapot to pour the tea into their cups. They each then scoop two sugar cubes into their cups.

Yesus - The amusing thing is, if God were Postmodern, even the Atheist would not be spared.

Yesus takes a sip from his cup.

Ahmed - This is truly an major existential problem my friend. One where pure reason seems to be unable to provide an answer, for man is not driven purely by reason.

Smiling Ahmed then takes a sip from his cup.

Yesus - I see you know Kant as well.

Ahmed - German made. Should be good. Yes?

Shaking his head in surrender, Yesus puts down his cup and reaches for a Turkish sweetcake.

Ahmed - Jokes aside. I guess the best way forward is that we learn to be contented where we are and live in harmony. But whenever there are differences there is bound to be conflict.

Ahmed sighs heavily.

Ahmed - Nothing is ever easy.

Yesus munches on his sweetcake and swallows.

Yesus - It has perhaps reached a singularity at this point. Either we all live by learning to live with each other or we die together.

Ahmed - Yes indeed.

Ahmed reaches for a sweetcake as well, while they sit back and share the sheesha in a carpet shop in Jerusalem.

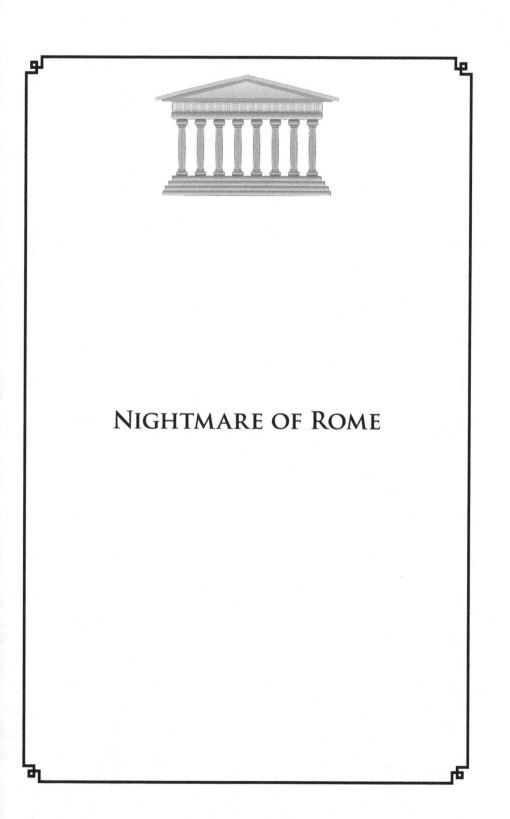

Nightmare of Rome

FOREWORD

*R*ome was not built overnight. Governance is never easy. Woe to those who govern for their task is never easy. Especially in providing guidance for their people. In the process some are able to maintain a facade of political correctness and some become tyrants. The challenges they face can sometimes be overwhelming.

Ideals are often used to keep us grounded but sometimes when different ideals clash they become no more ideals but tools which bring forth oppression. Dreams become nightmares.

Such, I hope, is a tale that paints such a picture.

Sitted on a lonely bed on a hot night is a man with ruffled hair and heavy laden eyes. He is unable to fall asleep as the same thoughts continue to cycle through his mind. Beads of sweat spotting his forehead, he stares at the floor just below his knees.

Many sleepless nights has he suffered and yet he is unable to shake himself from the paranoia that continues to haunt him. The most powerful man of Rome and he yet feels powerless as feverish thoughts fill his head.

Flashes of his younger days pass by. He being adopted by his Uncle. Given a proper Greek education in philosophy, logic and the arts. Having dreams about the grandeur of Rome. The empire of empires. Spanning from the island of savages in the west to Babylon in the East and including Egypt in the South.

Taught, that it was through Alexander the Great that many cultures were brought together just like Great Babylon. Bonded together by a common language and culture which superseded the ones present in the lands that were conquered.

Such was the greatness of Rome which he knew of as a child.

Then he became Caesar, after the sudden death of his uncle when he was about seventeen, and was entrusted with the huge responsibility of governing this massive empire. From then on his world changed, he became like Atlas, having this huge weight on his shoulders and in order to navigate the politics of Rome he had to become Dionysius. Understanding the desires of the people around him tipped the scales in his favour.

Rome was not built overnight but preserving its greatness requires a sustained effort so that its flame does not die out.

He stands up and proceeds to walk towards the open courtyard beyond the room's entrance. He looks up at the sky searching for the moon, only to find the silhouettes of many clouds filling the night sky. He sighs as he crosses his hands behind his back.

Paranoia begins to grow in his mind again. He wonders "Is there really an Almighty God?".

This new religion that has arisen because of Jesus the Christ, that he has heard of since he was a child, continues to trouble his mind. This man whom they call a great teacher, a man of peace, a god who died and came back from the dead. Who had many disciples that brought along with them many miracles which rival those of the Greek gods. Healing the sick and the demon-possessed, bringing the dead back to life and speaking in strange languages that foreigners can understand.

Such a report has never been recorded except in the stories of Homer. So many testify to these reports and the great "teachings" of Jesus.

These "teachings" of Jesus they are many. Some of them even contradicting each other. Especially the part that Jesus died because of persecution by the Pharisees, for the sins of men, and yet sacrifices still had to be made for sins. Or food which the Jews cannot eat also cannot be eaten by gentiles who convert to Christianity. This being hearsay from the Sadducees who still remained in Rome after the purge by his Uncle.

So many contradictions arise as he digs further into this mystery. One of the biggest contradictions being the Pharisees in Jerusalem, the ones who had Christ crucified, were reported to have set up a Council in Jerusalem. Declaring that all believers have to adhere to the Laws of Moses as Christ is a Jew, the Son of David. That scripture is from the Jews.

All this following reports about how the Spirit of God came upon the believers in Jerusalem and resulted in a wave of reported miracles that have spread throughout the empire.

This then led to a great conflict within Rome. A debate arose as to how "Christians" are to be treated under Roman law as the miracles were attracting a large following for this new religion.

For, if the Council in Jerusalem is to hold, under the auspices of the Temple, which had already been provided for prior to the coming of Christ then all "Christians" would no longer be under Roman law but under Temple law.

Some suggested, especially the Sadducees, that perhaps the Temple could be shifted to Rome. Some even suggested that perhaps Rome should change its ways, seeing that the teachings of Jesus were good. Especially the heavy handed methods utilised by Caesar.

Such was the nightmare that Rome faced and it continues now under his reign.

The greatness of Rome faced extinction should the Temple gain a foothold. Even if the teachings of Christ mainly spoke of peace he did not trust the Pharisees nor the Sadducees. Especially their criticisms of Rome as he was aware of their conniving ways. Rome can never be maintained by the teachings of Christ nor the Laws of Moses.

Calls continued to be made in the Senate for change, even from his allies. Affected by the teachings of Christ and politics in Jerusalem. But in his heart he knows that he must never lose Rome. The dream of Rome must be preserved at all cost.

He must continue to stay true to his course. The persecution of Christians have to continue. He has played with the idea of destroying the Temple in Jerusalem but he fears the backlash that might arise in Rome. He must now find a way to put the Temple and Jews in bad light. Much has he to achieve in order to bring this to pass while still maintaining his position in Rome.

Sweat flows down from his forehead. His hands tremble at the thought of what he has to do. He then clasps his hands, raising them as he looks up towards the starless night sky. Pursing his lips he then swears "By Jupiter! I will do this. I will be strong."

CONFESSIONS

FOREWORD

*I*t is perfect to be imperfect. However, sometimes imperfections are not the things we should be focusing on but the intent. Things done with proper intent though imperfect are probably fine. But things done with improper intent, no matter how right it seems to turn out can become a millstone hanging around a person's neck.

Perhaps the Catholic practice of confessions does have its place in our imperfect world. Even better if it were possible for us to confess our wrong intents in the afterlife.

The tale below involves three friends and how it might be like if confession were allowed in the afterlife.

Characters:

Gabriel Garcia Marquez (Mexican writer, 1982 Nobel Prize in Literature)

Pablo Neruda (Chilean writer, 1971 Nobel Prize in Literature)

Jorge Luis Borges (Argentinean writer)

[In the Sistine Chapel of Rome in front of its alter wall where Michaelangelo's fresco of *"Il Giudizio Universale"* - *"Universal Judgement"* stands]

Sunlight, from the upper windows, illuminates the tranquil silence within the Sistine Chapel. Three translucent figures stand before the alter wall. Standing just in front of it is Gabriel, on his right is Pablo and on the left is Borges. They look as if they had just arrived and were looking at each other like old friends who have not seen each other for a long time. Although Borges seemed to be looking a little awkward in their presence.

Gabriel was the first to speak.

Gabriel - Hello my fellow brothers. It has been a long time since we have seen each other. Afterall I was among the last to depart.

Pablo - Indeed. I was first among us. In very violent and tragic circumstances.

Borges - [In a meek voice] Very sorry about that Pablo. Intentional though it was but I have come to realise that it was a tragic miscalculation on my part.

Pablo - Apology accepted. One should not take vengeance beyond the grave. Unless of course it is the final day as painted in the picture before us.

Borges - [Laughing hesitantly] Yes. Agreed.

Gabriel - Let bygones be bygones. I did just that.

Borges - And you did help make it better.

A moment of silence passed between the three comrades. The air was still within the Sistine Chapel.

Pablo - We did share a dream once. A grand one indeed.

Borges - We all wrote about it in some way or another. A grand dream it was.

Gabriel - One where despite our differences in culture and ideals we could still actually achieve harmony together as a race.

Borges looked pensively at the alter wall.

Borges - Its beginning was in some sense simple. After the second world war everyone realised that we do not want to fight another war on such a grand scale. The most important concern for every common man was bread and butter issues.

Pablo looked at Borges and smirked. Then added.

Pablo - Indeed. The ideal we shared was for every man in every nation being able to put bread on the table for himself and his family.

Gabriel - [Shaking his head] But of course one problem was that all things were never equal. The divide between the rich and poor will always be there. Simply because resources are seldom evenly distributed.

Pablo - The other looming problem was that there were two rising global ideals, Communism and Democracy, which could potentially create strife among the many nations. Communism was of course more popular simply because it did not have the colonialistic baggage that major democratic countries had.

Borges - But we had the advantage because of our mature enterprises. This was also a draw for the people in other nations.

Pablo - True. But more true among the middle-class, those above and the elite of the country since they are responsible for most of the economic factories in their countries.

Gabriel - However, in the end every country had to make a choice. Some made it naturally while some made theirs after some struggle. Yet our dream could have been achieved if we could have learnt to live in peace.

Pablo - You mean if only other countries did not meddle in the affairs of other countries?

Suddenly Pablo's eyes slant towards Borges.

Borges - [Nodding in agreement] I have come to a deep realisation of what both of you said. I am truly sorry that I have criticised you so strongly at times Pablo. Your country included. Learning to live in peace, I have come to realise, is to also be able to accept people, and countries alike, for what they are. There will always be differences.

Gabriel - Sadly, the world still has not reached such a stage yet. Even when Communism is technically dead. As you mentioned Borges, there will always be differences. It is these differences that continue to create points of conflict.

Borges - If only we could discuss things rationally and not push our own personal agendas upon others.

Pablo's right eyebrow twitches up at Borge's comment.

Pablo - Another confession my friend?

Borges - [Nodding his head contritely] Yes.

Gabriel - Yet when I departed, the world I left was a postmodern one. One where no single truth dominates but many. A world filled with many differences and learning to handle its pluralistic reality.

Pablo & Borges - [In unison] A challenge indeed.

All three then looked down in silence as they pondered upon what they had said.

Pablo - We fought much then did we not.

Borges - Yes. But I have come to wonder what did we truly fought for. At the end of the day both Communism and Democracy believed in rights of the common man. Both believe that oppression is wrong. Yet in the end both ended being the oppressors.

Gabriel - True. As Communism evolved, in order to drive back the colonialistic objectives of Democracy some strains became violent and oppressive. While for Democracy, in its blind drive for economic expansion, turns a blind eye to the ills of many nations. Apartheid in Africa being one of them. Political control and manipulation being another.

Borges - Vietnam is another example of the mistakes of Democracy.

Gabriel - But yet at the core of it all both ideologies are the same. Just that they have very different economic models and their political leaders have differing objectives. Our fight was actually about almost anything but the ideologies themselves once you look pass the propaganda.

Both Pablo and Borges nod in unison. Gabriel then gave a wide smile as he looked at the both of them.

Borges - Most importantly, was the discovery of black gold. It was the lubricant of our grand dream. Yet the estacy for gold is something that can turn many people mad. Me probably included.

Pablo - [Smiles slyly] Lubricant?

Borges - [Returning a sly smile] Yes. A lubricant. Do you not remember bread on every man's table?

Pablo - Ah. Yes. Of course.

Borges - We could have achieved what I had initially termed "Tion" in "Ficciones". A higher order of existence. [Pauses for a moment] If only we could have lived in peace.

Gabriel - Yes. The rise in technological advancement and the need for electricity makes black gold a truly lucrative resource. Much which is found in the Middle East. At the end of the day if proper trade relations were set up, flow of money and goods can easily move around the world to provide for the common man in every nation.

Borges - Like now?

Gabriel - It is much better now but sadly politics can still interfere with trade relations and there are some parts of the world that are still in turmoil where there is no proper governance to provide proper trade relations which would properly benefit its people. Plus the game of economics has also become much more complex. Battles are no more just fought on the battlefield but also on the economic scale.

Borges - Looks like much still has not changed. Similar in many ways but perhaps with different threats?

Gabriel - Not really. Much has changed and improved. But the threats are similar albeit they now term it as "assymetric".

Pablo - What?

Gabriel - We had two big powers in the past. Communism and Democracy. Both are large powers thus it is symmetric.

Pablo - So now one is small and the other is large? Is that worse?

Gabriel - Not really. Well... Its complicated but the one that is small is the adversary.

Pablo & Borges - [Both raise their eyebrows] So the world is much better?

Gabriel - Well in some sense but with the rise in technology and the sciences there is much harm that the assymetric threat can do. Especially when many of them are hidden among the elite and powerful.

Pablo - So that means world events can sometimes be not within the control of the common man? Elites and powerful included.

Gabriel - Yes.

Borges - Just like what happened to Chile. When you died. [Eyes looking at Pablo]

Pablo - [Laughing sardonically] A tragedy indeed. Glad you owned up to it.

Borges - I must admit. The levers of power within my reach were too tempting. You know why I changed "Ficciones" to "Labyrinth". I turned our dreams into a trap. A trap within my control. Pinochet had no choice but to act as he did.

Pablo - Well played though.

Gabriel - But it did something to you didn't it.

Borges - Yes. It did. The trap I had constructed was my hope which later transformed into a nighmare. A nightmare I could never wake from. I became trapped in my own labyrinth. I realised, albeit later, just like you that the world after 1973 was not becoming better but probably worse. Especially for the common man.

Gabriel - I know. You died a brokened man. Someone who had to continue to sing the same story even though you knew it was pointless.

Pablo then placed a hand over Borges's shoulders.

Pablo - All is over and done my friend. No one is perfect.

Gabriel then joins in to stand on the other side of Borges. Putting a hand round his shoulders as well as the three of them look up towards the alter wall.

The Key

Where art thou?

Such a beautiful and horrible sight all at once.

To hold ye in my hands is to hold both heaven and hell.

The many doors that thou is able to open and close.

That many seek to possess you.

Such a beautiful and horrible sight all at once.

Where art thou?

BERLIN FARCE

FOREWORD

*F*air is foul and foul is fair: Hover through the fog and filthy air.

Such is the confusion we face when ideals clash. But sometimes all we end up with is parody and we wonder why we had made such a big fuss in the first place.

In the end, is it really about ideals that we are fighting over? Or is there more to it?

[In the radio broadcasting studio of Berlin's Broadcasting Centre]

Radio Jock 1 - Good morning everyone. If you just tuned in today's weather forecast is going to be a bright sunny day.

Radio Jock 2 - Yes indeed. Just great, as today is a special day.

Radio Jock 1 - 8th of May 2014! A day for celebration! Woo hoo!

Radio Jock 2 - Hahaha... I see you are really hyped up today.

Radio Jock 1 - Of course! Today marks the end of World War 2. When Nazi Germany officially surrendered unconditionally. Its "Victory in Europe Day".

Radio Jock 2 - You know that means we lost don't you?

Radio Jock 1 - Yes. Of course. But we can still celebrate it right! As it marks the end of an oppressive regime. It's a day to celebrate liberation!

Radio Jock 2 - Haha... Yes. In some sense it marks a political revolution for Germany.

Radio Jock 1 - But the path that we had to take was still going to be a rocky one.

Radio Jock 2 - True. We had to go through a second revolution of sorts before we got to where we are today.

Radio Jock 1 - Ah yes. The famous 1989 collapse of the Berlin Wall. Marking the end of another oppressive regime. Communism.

Radio Jock 2 - Like you said my fellow comrade. A day to celebrate liberation.

Radio Jock 1 - Haha... Very funny. Now to our fellow listeners our next song is titled "Dream" by the Cranberries. Enjoy.

["Dream" is being broadcast. Radio Jocks are currently off the airwaves.]

Radio Jock 1- I have always found this day quite amusing.

Radio Jock 2 - So do I.

Radio Jock 1 - We in Germany all know that Nazism stood for National Socialism and Hitler's party was legitimately elected into office by an overwhelming landslide victory. And the amusing thing is that Communism is also a strain of Socialism.

Radio Jock 2 - Haha... The only difference is that the Nazi party did not follow the economic model of collectivism practiced by Russia but instead decided to maintain a capitalistic model. Allowing for private ownership of enterprises.

Radio Jock 1 - And today, in the name of liberation, we celebrate the fall of these 2 regimes or political ideals. But you do realise that there is a deeper joke here.

Radio Jock 2 - Oh yes! Only a Berliner would recognise it. [Sniggers] Especially once you have understood that both Communism and Democracy actually respect the fact, that all men should have rights, as an ideal. The only difference being their economic ideals. One is, respectively, collectivistic and the other capitalistic.

Radio Jock 1 - Ergo there is simply not much difference between Communism and Democracy as ideals for proper governance.

Radio Jock 2 - Which also means [sniggering again] Nazism is the equivalent of our modern day Democracy.

[Both burst out laughing]

Radio Jock 1 - No. This is better. Current day Democracy is a form of Neo-Nazism. The old one hates Jews but the new one loves them.

[Both burst out laughing again]

Radio Jock 2 - Oh. The song's going to end.

Radio Jock 1 - Oops. Better get ready to get on air.

[The song "Dream" fades out]

Radio Jock 1 - To those who just tuned in that was "Dream" by the Cranberries.

Radio Jock 2 - Today is going to be a bright sunny day. To those driving please drive safely.

Radio Jock 1 - Think I am going to find a good spot of grass somewhere later and just sit down and enjoy my lunch.

Radio Jock 2 - I might just join you too! Oh yes. There is also going to be a celebration parade later on somewhere at the Brandenburg Gate plaza. Think it's going to be around noon.

Radio Jock 1 - Ah yes! There you go people. Hope to see you all there as well later.

Radio Jock 2 - By the way you mentioned earlier that today is a special day for us to celebrate liberation. But don't you think we should also be celebrating something else today?

Radio Jock 1 - What do you mean?

Radio Jock 2 - How about love?

Radio Jock 1 - Love?

Radio Jock 2 - Yes. Love. What else? It's also a day to celebrate the crumbling of political walls and boundaries that prevent us from being one big family. One human race.

Radio Jock 1 - Hmm... I guess you are right on that. Haha... So to everyone out there, let today be another Valentine's day for you! Buy some flowers and chocolates to express your heart-felt love.

Radio Jock 2 - Coincidentally we have just the right song lined up. Coming next is "I Do Believe In Love" by Katie Melua. Enjoy!

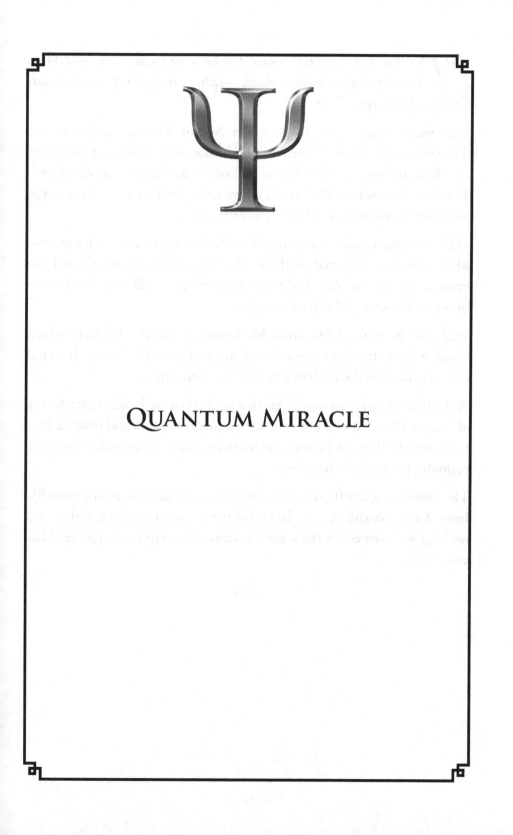

QUANTUM MIRACLE

"The Wheel of Time turns, and Ages come and pass." Wheel of Time Series by Robert Jordan, physics graduate from *The Citadel* a South Carolina Military College.

1927 was a time in the midst of an Age of Reason. Similar to the Babylonian Age where Mathematical advances were made and similar to the Hellenisation Age when Greek Philosophy and Logic were developed. The Age of Reason in 1927 could derive its beginnings as far back as the Renaissance, the period of Enlightenment in Europe.

1927 saw a crowning achievement of our Modern Age where Fact is supreme, while values are relegated to the hidden private spheres of life, and the mysteries of Nature plus all the problems of life would soon be resolved through Science and Rational thought.

1927 saw the birth of Quantum Mechanics. A branch of Science which would usher in the technological revolutions of the 20th Century. It would then also catalyse the birth of a new Postmodern Age.

Yet in all its glory lies an irony. One that has to do with the diametric duality of Nature. One that reinforces the coexistence of, Reason and Irrationality; Logic and the Illogical; Science and Miracles; that it is natural for diametric opposites to coexist in harmony.

The following scientific article is a farce that tries to illustrate the scientific basis of such coexistence. At the end of the article, should you understand nothing with respect to the scientific ideas being expressed, just read the conclusion.

*****

Formulas and concepts used in Schrodinger's assumptions to formulate the final Schrodinger's Wave Equation resulting in the *Quantum Miracle* of the 20th Century

Abstract

Quantum Mechanics
by Richard P. Feynman

Electrons, when they were first discovered, behaved exactly like particles or bullets, very simply. Further research showed, from electron diffraction experiments for example, that they behaved like waves. As time went on there was a growing confusion about how these things really behaved ---- waves or particles, particles or waves? Everything looked like both.

This growing confusion was resolved in 1925 or 1926 with the advent of the correct equations for quantum mechanics. *Now we know how the electrons and light behave... It behaves like nothing you have seen before.*

There is one simplication at least. ***Electrons behave in this respect in exactly the same way as photons;*** *they are both screwy, but in* ***exactly in the same way...***

The difficulty really is psychological and exists in the perpetual torment that results from your saying to yourself, ***"But how can it be like that?"*** *which is a reflection of uncontrolled but utterly vain desire to see it in terms of something familiar... There was a time when the newspapers said that only twelve men understood the theory of relativity. I do not believe there ever was such a time. There might have been a time when only one man did, because he was the only guy who caught on, before he wrote his paper. But after people read the paper a lot of people understood the theory of relativity in some way or other, certainly more than twelve. On the other hand,* ***I think I can safely say that nobody understands quantum mechanics.*** *So do not take the lecture too seriously, feeling that you really have to understand in terms of some model what I am going to describe, but just relax and enjoy it...*

Nobody knows how it can be like that.

Richard P. Feynman, The Messenger Lectures, 1964, MIT

Note: Words in bold are for emphasis.

Introduction

Two of the great scientific triumphs of the 20th Century is the birth of General Relativity and Quantum Mechanics.

General Relativity helped complete our scientific understanding about the things in the ordinary world that we are able to touch, feel and observe. It completed the scientific description of the ordinary world.

Quantum Mechanics allowed us to understand the world of the atom. It enabled us to understand a world which cannot be touched, felt or observed directly with the naked eye, even with the most powerful of microscopes.

General Relativity

The physical predictions made by the theory of General Relativity can be observed in Nature and through our interactions with it. For example, our accurate calculations of rocket, satellite or planet trajectories and observations showing that light bends during astrological observations.

In short all that can be found in General Relativity, be it during its formulation by Einstein or after it has been formulated, can be *observed*! Be it physically by our eyes or heuristically in the mind's eye.

Quantum Mechanics

However, the atomic world that Quantum Mechanics describes is not observable by our eyes at all. Whatever idea we have about the atomic universe is all based simply on educated imagination.

Here the importance of man's imagination cannot be stressed any more than Sesame Street does. *Imagination* is the only thing we have to grasp the atomic world.

This fantastical atomic world that we try to understand, apart from atoms and molecules, also consists of photons which are mostly Electromagnetic (EM) Radiation.

It is in attempting to imagine this fantasy universe that Schrodinger finally came up with his namesake Wave Equation that brought about the birth of Quantum Mechanics which revolutionised the world in the 20th Century.

Revolutions that came about include the computer age which came with the invention of the transistor, semi-conductor, logic gates, etc.

The Nuclear Age was also ushered in. This includes nuclear energy, weapons and even atomic colliders like CERN's Hadron Collider.

The wonders of this unobservable atomic universe is now seemingly within our reach.

Genesis of Schrodinger's Wave Equation

Schrodinger was perturbed by many recent discoveries prior to his own discovery of the Schrodinger Wave Equation.

First of these was Max Planck's assumption that the energy carried by absorbed and emitted EM Radiation was quantised in fixed energy packets. Max Planck had done it out of desperation to find the correct mathematical equation to describe blackbody radiation as it was the only way to avoid the unobservable prediction of an ultra-violet catastrophe where radiation in the ultra-violet region would spike to infinity.

Next was Einstein's Nobel Prize winning observation of the photoelectric effect that proved without a shadow of a doubt that EM Radiation, like light, is quantised.

$$E = h\nu$$

Fig 1. Equation stating energy of a photon. Observed from the Photoelectric Effect. (ν is the "frequency" of EM Radiation. h is "Planck's constant".)

Thirdly, was the de Broglie equations which were derived by combining the wave properties of waves with the particulate properties of EM Radiation, described by Figure 1.

$$\lambda = h/p \quad p = \hbar k$$
$$f = E/h \quad E = \hbar\omega$$

Fig 2. Equivalence of Wave - Particle variables (By de Broglie)

In some sense these three factors were the main things flowing in Schrodinger's mind prior to his grand discovery.

Schrodinger was probably already assuming that in the atomic universe, or perhaps even throughout all of Nature, matter exists in a dual state of being both wave and particle.

A wave has wavelength, frequency and period. While a particle has momentum and energy. So what he now needs to mathematically frame the Quantum world, like how a Hamiltonian frames the dynamics of objects in the Physical world, is an equation that combines both wave and particle elements. These elements are listed in Figure 2.

Thus he first sought to do this with the classical wave equations but was unsuccessful. (He tried to incorporate the particulate-quantise nature of waves into the equation.)

$$\frac{\partial^2 u}{\partial t^2} = c^2 \nabla^2 u$$

Fig 3. Classical Wave Equation taking into account a **wave's spatial evolution** with respect to time & space (c is a fixed constant. For EM-Waves c is the speed of light. u is a wave function.)

It was only much later, about less than a year later, around 1925 that he finally thought that the equation could perhaps follow the form of a Classical Hamiltonian. But with wave and particle-quantisation elements in it.

$$\hat{H} = \hat{T} + \hat{V}$$

Fig 4. Example of a Classical Hamiltonian which accounts for the kinetic energy (T) and potential energy (V) of a system.

$$i\hbar \frac{\partial}{\partial t} \Psi = \hat{H} \Psi$$

$$i\hbar \frac{\partial}{\partial t} \Psi(\mathbf{r}, t) = \left[\frac{-\hbar^2}{2m} \nabla^2 + V(\mathbf{r}, t) \right] \Psi(\mathbf{r}, t)$$

Fig 5. The Schrodinger Wave Equation incorporating a **Hamiltonian-like** right-side (H represents a Hamiltonian Operator that when expanded looks like the right-side of the equation below. The Hamiltonian involves only spatial differentials. Ψ is a wave function.) with a time differential on the left-side. This takes into account the **evolution of a wave's energy** with respect to time and space.

So essentially Figure 5 illustrates the final result of this combination of wave and particle elements into a wave equation. So what Schrodinger's equation is saying is that the energy value that comes out of differentiating a wave function should be the same for a first-order time differential and a second-order spatial differential. This happens to work fine with Euler's Formula $e^{i(kx+wt)}$ which also, upon analysis of Maxwell's Equations for Classical Electromagnetic Radiation, is what a wave-function representing the photons of EM Radiation should be like.

$$\nabla \cdot \mathbf{E} = 0 \qquad \nabla \times \mathbf{E} = -\frac{\partial \mathbf{B}}{\partial t},$$

$$\nabla \cdot \mathbf{B} = 0 \qquad \nabla \times \mathbf{B} = \frac{1}{c^2}\frac{\partial \mathbf{E}}{\partial t}.$$

Fig 6. Maxwell's Equations for Classical Electromagnetic Radiation. Upon further analysis shows that Electric and Magnetic radiation are orthogonal to each other, in EM Radiation, and can therefore be combined and expressed in Euler's Formula.

Note that up to this point, it was actually photons that was in Schrodinger's mind when formulating his Wave Equation. *V* (electric-charge potential energy) was still not present in the Wave Equation. Also note that classically no one has used wave functions (e.g. Euler's Formula) with a Hamiltonian which contextually was meant to describe a particulate system.

Quantum Miracle

The Schrodinger Wave Equation was published in 1926. Subsequently it was vigorously tested and analysed for use in illuminating how an electron in a Hydrogen atom interacts with the proton in its nucleus.

The strange thing here was that almost all the secrets the Hydrogen atom held were reproduced through the Schrodinger Wave Equation. Especially with regard to the spectral energetics that would be produced should the electron in the atom be excited.

In short, it was a resounding success as theoretical mathematical data matched physical experimental data. It was a theoretical triumph for Physics.

However, here is the strange bit that made the triumph into a conundrum and perhaps even a miracle of sorts. It was later found through further analysis of the data that photons are Bosons while electrons are Fermions.

Technically this means that photons follow Bose-Einstein statistics and electrons follow Fermi-Dirac statistics. **This simply means photons and electrons are two very different species of quantum objects. Futhermore, if you consider things further, photons are totally unaffected by electric or magnetic fields but this is completely opposite for electrons which hold a single negative charge.**

Note that this is a crucial point as it means that when Schrodinger first formulated his Wave Equation, with photons in mind, it actually works for electrons as well. And this is what Feynman means when he says **"But how can it be like that?"** followed by **"I think I can safely say that nobody understands quantum mechanics."**

Because nobody knows how it can be like that.

The birth of Quantum Mechanics is actually a Miracle. It was purely by sheer luck that Schrodinger got it correct. Especially when you realise that the initial Wave Equation, when photons were being considered, did not have V (electric-charge potential energy) present in it.

It was only when considering how the electron interacts with the proton in a Hydrogen atom that the potential V was included to account for the electric potential energy of the positively charged proton.

Conclusion

With the subsequent advent of "Computer Technology" (e.g. transistors, micro-processors, RAM, etc.), "Nuclear Technology" and "The Standard Model" in physics after the birth of Quantum Mechanics, we can without a shadow of a doubt conclude that Schrodinger's Wave Equation *works!*

Because all other later advances in our understanding of the atomic world, like Dirac's Wave Equations, Quantum Field Theory (QFT), Quantum Electrodynamics (QED) or the still in progress Quantum Chromodynamics (QCD) are derived from Schrodinger's Wave Equation.

However, the "Fact" that it works is in itself a miracle, if you believe in supernatural intervention, or a pure stroke of luck. An inexplicable quirk in the history of Man.

This "Fact" also does suggest the bi-polar or dualistic side of Nature. That there is always two sides to every coin. That perhaps multiple perspectives or truths do exist instead of the singular perspective that the Modern Framework holds to.

It also shows that diametrically opposite views, like the rational and irrational, can coexist harmoniously in Nature. Without any conflict. Hinting at the foundations of how a harmonious postmodern or pluralistic world can be developed.

Farcical as this scientific article may sound but one cannot avoid the ramifications of this "Fact".

REFERENCES

1. Introduction to Quantum Mechanics, David J. Griffiths

2. http://en.wikipedia.org/wiki/General_relativity

3. http://en.wikipedia.org/wiki/Erwin_Schr%C3%B6dinger

4. http://en.wikipedia.org/wiki/Mass%E2%80%93energy_equivalence

5. http://en.wikipedia.org/wiki/Wave_equation

6. http://en.wikipedia.org/wiki/Matter_wave

7. http://en.wikipedia.org/wiki/Schr%C3%B6dinger_equation

8. http://en.wikipedia.org/wiki/Euler%27s_formula

Modern Conundrum

FOREWORD

*W*e now live in the 21ˢᵗ Century. On the edge of Modernity and on the cusp of Postmodernism. A world with many world-views and sub-world-views.

We live in truly pluralistic times. Freedom of thought and choice has brought us to this stage. The worst thing that could happen is you would either feel trapped or confused. Trapped if you believe in the Modern mindset that truth is Singular. Because the framework with which you use to view the world is incomplete, inadequate to describe the reality that you live in.

Confused if you are a Postmodernist, as you believe that truth is pluralistic, that you require different perspectives to properly frame reality. But because there are so many perspectives flowing around, you find it challenging to piece them together into a coherent whole. Even if you appreciate abstract art.

However one thing does stick out of this Modern Conundrum, that is the need for conflict. Conflict is inevitable in such a reality. Differences always give birth to conflict. Therefore what is really required in such an age, or perhaps every age in the history of Man, is a framework for conflict resolution.

Yet one might argue that there would then, probably, be a plethora of conflict resolution frameworks to be used. So which do we use? Is there a way perhaps to simplify the problem?

Perhaps the simplification can be found in the desired final outcome of all conflicts. Especially after going through two world wars in the preceding century alone.

[Anywhere in a University or a place of learning]

Prof - Good day to you.

Student - Good day to you as well.

Prof - What brings you to me this day?

Student - I bring with me many questions. Please I need your help.

Prof - Sure. By all means fire away your questions.

Student - Do you think we live in Modern or Postmodern times now?

Prof - In between times. As you know, I myself am openly Postmodernist. However, that is only my personal view. As you know our reality is a co-creation of every person's observation and interpretation of the world. This is what we could call observer created reality. I am after all also Democratic.

Student - Hmm... So that means we are in the early stages of Postmodernity but because not everyone accepts this world-view we are somewhere in-between.

Prof - Yes.

Student - I do concur on the need to be pluralistic when trying to understand the world we live in. But does not this mean anything goes? If anything goes then which framework or world-view should I choose to piece together my personal view of reality? It just seems so very confusing!

Prof - Understand your frustration. But it still can be done. The thing is to be able to accept all views and if they contradict, you are to question why they contradict each other. Since each view arises out of its own private context, you would then need to dig deeper to understand the private context behind each view.

Student - Doesn't this mean that I have to dig into everyone's private life?

Prof - In some sense, yes. But there are always views that converge and aggregate. So they help you reach a certain estimate or average in your conclusion. See part of being a Postmodernist is understanding the Uncertainty Principle. That many things in Nature are seldom *completely* for certain. Partly because we are also not omniscient or all-knowing.

Student - Therefore all of us are forced, in a sense, into a stance of humility when conversing with one another in a dialogue.

Prof - Correct. I see you remembered a comment I made during one of my lectures.

Student - However, what are we to do if no one wants to back down during a debate? In the end there would still be conflict. A fight would probably ensue with probably no end in sight as well.

Prof - Ah yes. That can happen. Very much a worst case scenario. I guess in this case one has to take note of the mental state of the parties involved. Are they entering into the debate just to create conflict or are they trying to resolve certain issues.

Student - I see. But as you mentioned before that due to the two world wars in the 20th Century the aggregate mental state of most people in developed countries is to avoid conflict. Avoidance of conflict becomes one of the levers we can use for leverage in a debate. "A fight to avoid a fight." You mentioned.

Prof - [Smiling broadly] Yes again. In the end the debate does have to end amicably otherwise it would end with a bad taste in the mouth of the parties involved. So in general, whether conflict is avoided or not a "fight" still has to occur for the matter to be resolved.

Student - But what if some do not wish to fight?

Prof - Then their views would simply be dominated by the party that fights. Taking a backseat in the whole debate.

Student - Why is it that conflict or "fighting" is always involved in every part of Man's history. When will Man ever learn not to fight?

Prof - My friend. Man will always have to fight. There will always be things to fight over. Be it naturally occurring or artificially created. The truth is that we must at the end of the day learn how to fight. But not fighting is also sometimes a mode of attack and not necessarily cowardice.

Student - Examples?

Prof - I am an Atheist but I have read the Bible on my own and I find that even though Jesus is touted to be a man of peace but if you read his sayings very carefully in the context of the political situation of his time you will find that he is indeed a Teacher of the highest order. He frames his speeches in such a manner that, though sounding peaceful, bites and resolves conflict all at once. I am quite sure that his opponents are aware of this.

Student - Erm... I am a Christian but I have never thought of Jesus in such a manner. Any other examples perhaps?

Prof - You heard of Tai-Chi? Or perhaps you have seen the recent Ip-Man film starring Donnie Yen?

Student - Yes.

Prof - I am no martial arts exponent but I have read up on some of the philosophies behind them. Tai-Chi in its original form is formless, it has no style yet its forms flow like fluid water. This is because there is never a one size fits all style in conflict. Every conflict setting has its own context thus the fighter then has to conform to the context to be effective. Just like how water takes the shape of whatever cup it is poured into.

Then there is the Yong-Chun style created by Ip-Man but when Ip-Man fights it is not to create conflict it is to resolve conflict or to avoid a greater conflict. There is also Ip-Man's disciple, Bruce Lee.

Student - Oh... I have heard of him. Was a Hong Kong movie star who directed and starred in many action films.

Prof - Yes. Bruce Lee incorporated both the philosophy of Tai-Chi and the philosophy of his teacher into his life and martial arts. He wanted to represent what it means to fight. Even in his movies.

Student - What? I never thought Bruce Lee in such a complicated way. I thought he was just a movie star.

Prof - Hahaha... Well every person in this world is complex. Never assume that anyone is a mere simpleton. So do you grasp what I have been trying to tell you so far?

Student - I guess... I will need time to do more readings and digest what you have said.

Prof - Haha... Not to worry. The essay I will be asking you all to write has no right or wrong answer. What I am looking for is how you think and justify your views in the essay.

Student - [Smiling back] Thanks professor! It has been great chatting with you.

[Student leaves]

Epilogue

N ow comes the end. Or what seems to be an end. There is a saying that the end is just a new beginning. At least till the Wheel of Time is brokened.

One thing is broken however. My mind. Voices in my mind have guided me in my writings. Including an eleventh story titled "Screwloose conversations with Screwtape" which I had scrapped as it was giving me the shivers.

If you are not in the know, Screwtape is suppose to be a fictional demon of C.S Lewis but again there is a saying that to be on the safe side always believe in the Devil. Thus my reason for pulling the eleventh story out. It scared me. And if I had included it in its totality I think it would scare you too. For the eleventh story would have brought a spine chilling close to the first ten...

So in the end I went what the heck! Why not make it the title! I need my catharsis.

In "Screwloose conversations with Screwtape" I converse with voices in my head. I vaguely heard the name Screwtape. But that was not what scared me. It was what the voice portended that freaked me out. It was trying to tell me that outcropping from the stories was a current day existentialistic catastrophe of immense proportions that is all centred upon the question, what if there is a God? I am not considering the many gods scenario as the gods are generally quite benign therefore, again, what if there was only one God?

Firstly you would have to ask, of all the Monotheistic religions, which God is the right one. But Screwtape gave me a doomsday scenario. He told me that due to the *Jerusalem Paradox* and *Modern Conundrum* a *Labyrinthe* for humanity has been set up. This ruse is a result of removing from Man's mind important monuments, as in *Necropolis*, of Man's history. Therefore allowing for his *Cult* to take advantage of Man's ignorance to produce meaningless and farcical conflicts (e.g. The Berlin wall in 1961.) which make nightmares, similar to that of Rome's, a reality.

A reality which no amount of *Confession* nor Miracle of Science can save us from. For we are all connected and intertwined in this age of globalisation. All major monotheistic religions are involved in the *Jerusalem Paradox*. Thus we are all inexorably condemned and even if God should show us mercy through sacrificial proxy, like by having His Son die and suffer in our place, many will still fall away through lack of belief.

The Devil will indeed have his day. His eventual defeat would be met by the demise of many in conjunction with his many servants. Screwtape included of course.

This means even if I were to play safe there is a two-third chance that I got it wrong. Even if I got it right heaven would be a crummy place to be, knowing that most of the human race living around my lifetime would be in Hell, or at least some place far worst then Heaven.

Many cheers to you all who would be reading the stories. If there is any hope left well there is still one small voice in my Head for that. Although I am not too sure if it is not the same voice as Screwtape's. There is a saying that the Devil is the Father of Lies.

Yet foolishly it seems to say.

The Anti-Christ cannot win. The worse things get, the better. Simply because it would mean it ain't our fault if we do not believe. Unbelief is a result of things being really bad. So sit back and no worries. Enjoy the tales.

PART 2

Necronomicon

PROLOGUE - A TROUBLED MIND

"That is not dead which can eternal lie. And with strange aeons even death may die." is a rhyme from "The Call of Cthulhu". What it means, few can tell. But what it suggests is that even Death is mortal. Perhaps, when Christ the Redeemer does return Death would truly be put to the grave.

However, before such a time, one would have to learn to be satisfied with life even as the high cost of living is Death.

The *other* that is as certain as Death is the Devil. As the saying goes "always believe in the Devil". And it is a safe saying.

For I have been hearing voices. Voices that continue to resound in my head, telling me things which I know not to believe or to ignore. Because belief would lead to the worse of outcomes while to ignore would mean peril to our very existence.

Such compulsion I have yet to experience till now. What you are about to read is a result of these compulsions. Be it figments of my imagination or ramblings of a troubled mind I hope you can empathise with these dreams or nightmares.

REFLECTIONS ON GENESIS[2]

What better place to begin than Genesis? The first book in the bible that speaks of the creation and fall of Man. What whispers can one get from this part of human history? Apparently much.

Firstly what is Man? Need I say more on this well known subject? However what I am reconsidering, is what is Adam and Eve? What I am reconsidering is whether they are actually plural. Adam is the plural for first man while Eve is plural for first woman.

For it is mentioned in chapter one that God made the first animals of land, sea and air plurally. Many He made them and many of each kind. Therefore it would be safer to consider that when God made man on the sixth day he did not only make one of each gender.

Thus the Fall of Man involved more than one individual which brings me to my next reflection that is what did Man really do to fall from God's favour. The partaking of this forbidden fruit from the Tree of the Knowledge of Good and Evil was what brought about Man's downfall but most see it to be metaphorical so what act of Man does this image represent?

---

[2]   Note that it may not be apparent but after reading "Reflections on Genesis" you might want to find out more about Yggdrasil, The World Tree. Because the Tree of Life and the Tree of Knowledge of Good & Evil, when intertwined together, form the equivalent of Yggdrasil. For they are the Axis Mundi upon which the world revolves. The world turns because of the existence of Life and the dictates of Good & Evil.

Humorously, it is most definitely not sexual intercourse as in the very first chapter God already told man to multiply and fill the earth. What I have come to conclude upon reflection is that the image is about conflict. From the smallest between at least two individuals to that which is of a grand scale, namely War.

My reason is this, that the Tree of Knowledge can also be seen as a Tree of the Knowledge of Good and Bad or Knowledge of opposing thought. The Tree had already existed in the Garden thus being able to see the tree meant that Adam and Eve were already capable of conceptualising opposing thoughts. For man was also made in the image of God who already knows Good and Evil.

However opposing thoughts are probably fine. Like when one chooses an apple while another chooses an orange instead. But what makes opposing thoughts problematic is when one ascribes to them values of Good or Bad. As this could potentially create an environment that is fertile for conflict to occur.

This would then lead to a contest. A contest involving Will, physical strength and perhaps even physical possessions. These are all essential ingredients in any conflict. This also makes man like God as he is now able to exert influence and lordship over mankind as the victor would be able to dictate what is right and wrong.

This, I think, is the reason why the Serpent, that represents Satan, said that when you partake of the fruit you become like God. Not only knowing Good and Evil in the mind but also in deed.

So conflict, whether big or small becomes the fruit of opposing Knowledge. It is this fruit which Adam and Eve partook of that led to the fall of Man.

So it was probably conflict between woman and man followed by conflict between factions of Man that resulted in Man falling out of God's favour. Therefore it would mean that Man's Sin is his inability or lack of thereof to coexist in harmony.

This is perhaps why Jesus Christ said that in order to fulfill all the Laws in Scripture and by the Prophets one must be able to fulfil two conditions and that is to truly love God and to love ones neighbour as one loves yourself.

Thus when there is conflict the second condition would definitely not be met and the first condition would also not be met as it is a transgression of God's perfect will, since the beginning of creation, that Man is to live in harmony with one another. Transgression translates to disobedience and disobedience translates into no love for God.

This is what Christ came to save Man from. This is Christ's Raison D'etre. This is why Christ, during his time on earth, was a man of peace not war. This was the reason why Christ rejected proclaiming himself as King of the Jews despite being pressed, cajoled and ridiculed by the Pharisees. As he wanted to avoid a Jewish Roman conflict. Thus his eventual crucifixion. A crucifixion that also sought to remove another result of the birth of conflict. That is the removal of Shame through Christ's subsequent resurrection.

Shame is one of the results of conflict when you lose or when you are wrong for having caused the conflict. Then there is also Shame towards God for the destruction brought about to relationships, human bodies and physical materials which God had set in Harmony in his originally perfect World. Thus the metaphorical episode of shameful nakedness, in chapter three of the Book of Genesis.

THE GREAT SCHISM

So when relationships were damaged by conflict I think the mind of Man was also punished. Not only from shame but from a schism of the mind. I think when creation first started out, Man's mind was one with one another and with God. This is what a "spiritual relationship" is probably supposed to be.

Therefore, as if our minds were quantumly entangled, all man's thoughts were transparent to each other and man was meant to revel in that communion of the mind. In addition, Man's mind also shared communion with God's "mind".

However when Sin entered the World after the Fall of Man, our minds were fractured. Communion with God's "mind" was broken as Man had wilfully destroyed the harmonious perfection of creation. And the communion of the mind that Man shared with one another was also broken so that Man would fight less among themselves.

The Great Schism was punishment and also a conflict resolution process. For in the event of a large scale conflict how scary it would be if a faction of Man fought together as one big unit against another. It would be like two large Leviathans[3] striking at each other. Making the earth tremble with trepidation.

---

3   Thomas Hobbes wrote a book of the same name "Leviathan". It makes references to men acting in unison as a reflection of political will.

PRIMARY COLOURS OF MAN

It is therefore pertinent in the light of the violent trepidation that the earth faces in such a scenario that I have to mention the theory of Primary Colours. Mainly Red, Green and Blue. For they are essential to my future ramblings.

Note that in The Great Schism Man's mind was fractured. No more was Man of one mind with each other or God. However after Christ's resurrection the veil between Man's mind was torn and this was most probably during the day of Pentecost where there was the in-filling of the Holy Spirit. Thus for the many that came to believe in Christ communion was restored between their minds and with God.

This important event is not without precedence and continues on after Pentecost. But this restoration in the communion of minds is the crucial point that you must try to understand and grasp in order to understand the theory of Primary Colours.

Next important point to note is, as the saying goes "always believe in the Devil", thus even with the return of communion, the Devil can still be in the details. This is represented by the colour Red. Red represents men who have returned to communion but have retained their sense of ego and selfishness. Meaning even in the midst of communion they still perform acts that serve only their own purposes even when they contravene the sanctity of communion.

While the other two colours represent the believers who live life the best they know how in the midst of communion and the Reds. Blue represents those who see their lives having a higher purpose and do their best to work towards this higher purpose. And Green represents the simple and poor in spirit who share in this communion, being able to see a higher purpose to life, but choosing to live it simply for they are but simple folk.

Thus the Primary Colours represent the three main factions that share in the communion of the mind. Understanding this would be crucial to later developments for they would be the basis for my future ramblings.

Also note another two variations in colour. They are white and black. White is for someone who is able to have influence over all three colours for all three colours together make white. Like Jesus. While black is for those who are not part of the communion, they are in the absence of all colours. The average Joe of the human race. Also known respectfully as the Pillars of Creation.

Please seriously reflect upon the theory of Primary Colours before proceeding. More would probably be revealed as you read on.

AFTER THE FALL

After the Fall the violence of Sin has now entered the world. Man also now live in shame, from their exile from Eden, and also with a fractured mind. Yet in the little that is recorded in Genesis we know that the world after Man's dismissal from Eden, the new world, gradually fell back into Sin and violence[4].

It became so bad that God had to remake the world through the destruction of The Flood. The Flood was the first recorded demonstration that God was free to exact destruction on Man and Nature in order to usher in a new world. This demonstrates that God is truly Lord over all things and that he is not only a God of creation and love but also a fearsome God of destruction[5].

Yet after all things were made new after The Flood it began to turn sour again in the plains of Shinar where the Tower of Babel was built. A Tower which represented the gathering of Man united under one language. It represented the might of Man as one people and also the great folly that Man achieved as one people. For God descended and confused the languages of the people so that they would be forced to scatter and no longer stand united. The reason for God doing such a thing must have to do with the evil which Man is capable of when they stand united.

---

[4] Refer to Genesis 6:11.
[5] The only Hero recorded prior to The Flood is Enoch who ascended and did not see death for God took him away.

Such an earth shattering event occurred only about a hundred years after The Flood.[6] But God in his mercy had already promised, after The Flood, that the rainbow would represent his covenant with Man that he will never send a world-wide destruction like The Flood ever again. Thus in his wisdom he created chaos instead to break Man away from their Sin in Babel[7].

Depressing these primeval stories of Man may sound but it is inevitable because of Sin. However they do demonstrate God's sovereignty, in the myriad of actions that He is able to take to bring harmony back into the world.

---

[6]   This estimate was based on the time Peleg was born to Shem for it is written that the earth was divided during his time which seems to refer to the Babel episode.

[7]   Note that Babel interestingly can also be translated to mean chaos or disorder. Showing that God is not only a God of order but also of chaos. And also note that Nimrod was probably a Hero of the Babel episode in Shinar, which later became Babylon, as he was termed to be a mighty hunter for the Lord. Thus implying Nimrod worked with God to engineer the scattering of the people in Babel and became a Lord over those who remained in Shinar. This can be inferred from Babylonian archaeological finds where Nimrod was known as Nimrud in later Babylon and was venerated to be a hero.

MELCHIZEDEK

It is highly probable that despite the Great Schism God sometimes pulls down the veil for some chosen people. One of them is probably Melchizedek, King of Salem and Priest for God of the Most High. If there were others before him, from those who were recorded in Genesis, they would probably be Enoch and Nimrod among many others. For no man was ever meant to be a lonely island.

This chosen few probably enjoy communion with God's "mind" and perhaps even communion with other men. These chosen are what we can probably term prophets or men acting under God's direction. Thus validating the belief that God continues to commune with and use men for his purposes despite the Great Schism.

Note that this was before Israel. Before there were Jews. A chosen nation created by God.

The Patriarchs &
the Formation of Israel

This then brings us to the First Patriarch of Israel, also a chosen man of God, Abraham. God promised Abraham that he would make his name great among the nations and through him will come a great nation. And through Abraham shall the other people of the earth be blessed.

This is God referring to the future nation of Israel which would come forth from Abraham for it was with Abraham that the promise was first given. This was part of God's great plan during Abraham's lifetime.

From Abraham came forth the other patriarchs as well. In chronological order, they are Isaac then Jacob who was later known as Israel and who brought forth the father's of the twelve tribes of Israel. The patriarchs were chosen men of God and probably had communion with God and men.

Why they were chosen no one probably knows except by God's sovereign will. What they were chosen for is apparent, for the formation of the nation of Israel.

The nation, like its patriarchs, is chosen thus its people were also chosen therefore all Israelites enjoyed communion with God and among other fellow Israelites. They are probably the first nation to enjoy such a privilege of having the veil lifted as a people.

Thus they are able to act together as one big terrifying unit when they entered Canaan to bring God's judgement upon it and to conquer it. Imagine lightning fast reactions as a nation to changes in the battlefield simply because every combatant knows where everyone else is and what they are seeing or going through. It is simply telepathy at play. Such was the terrifying nature of Israel in battle in unison with God's guidance and divine help.

Thus was the nation of Israel raised in the land of Canaan, the land of milk and honey, to be a beacon of God's glory to the surrounding nations. So as to draw them into worship and communion with God, the God of Israel. This was probably part of God's Mission and part of it is for Him to be made known to Man so that communion between God and Man can be reinstated.

Failure of Israel

However, despite many high points in Israel's history as a nation, from the Judges to Kings like David and Solomon, Israel still failed in its mission. Its relationship with God varied from generation to generation. Even though it had a glorious history and communion with God it failed to always give God glory. At times they grow complacent and worshipped the idols of the surrounding nations for political, economic and social influence with these nations. Instead of pointing them to God Israel pointed them away for its own selfish reasons.

To be fair one cannot assume that everyone in the respective generations that failed were negligent towards God. After all the whole nation shared communion of the mind. This is where the Theory of Colour comes in. Most probably there were influential Reds in the generation that manipulated the Nation away from worshipping God and this were times when the Blues were weak in influence and the simple Greens were also pulled along for the ride.

This is probably what accounts for the rise and fall in Israel's relationship throughout different generations. Thus to mediate the problem God raised chosen people to punish and guide his people. They took the form of Judges, Prophets, Kings and occasionally people from the surrounding nations. Sadly towards the later part of Israel's history it performed badly and eventually the nation of Israel was obliterated by the Babylonians, during the reign of Nebuchadnezzar, with the razing of Jerusalem and its Temple. Many of its surviving people were then displaced to Babylon for integration into the empire.

Even when the Jews in Babylon were allowed to return to Jerusalem to rebuild it they did not remain faithful to God for long. The Reds among them started doing things that God did not like and even in Malachi, the last book of the Old Testament, God was unhappy with the priesthood of the rebuilt Temple in Jerusalem.

Even Judas Maccabeus was a small high point after Malachi. But he did in a way herald the coming of Jesus for he was from the line of David who took over the duties of the Temple in Jerusalem when he was ruler of the Jews. So like Jesus, he was a kingpriest, whereas traditionally priesthood and royalty were separate.

Subsequently, during the reign of Caesar Augustus, who was the Roman Emperor when Jesus was born, Jerusalem and its Temple came under the kingship of a Gentile Herod[8].

---

[8]   This means during the time of Jesus the Jews were ruled by a Gentile king and, at the same time, fell within the protection of the Roman Empire. Thus the political climate in Jerusalem is more complicated and layered involving the Pharisees of the Temple, Herod and the Roman governor.

ASSYRIA AND BABYLON

Due to Israel's folly, after King Solomon, it split into the Northern and Southern Kingdoms. The Southern Kingdom was made up of the largest tribe Judah and small tribe Benjamin while the rest of the tribes were in the Northern Kingdom.

The North mainly had bad kings while the South started off with relatively good kings. But when these kingdoms became rotten to the core, God had to pass a final judgement upon them with Assyria and Babylon being the swords of judgement fashioned by God to move against Israel.

Assyria was the sword of God's judgement against the Northern Kingdom of Israel while Babylon, which consumed Assyria later on in history, was the sword brought up against the remaining Southern Kingdom. And it was Babylon, as it is written in the Book of Jeremiah, that was the sword that gave the coup de grace that ended the existence of Israel as a nation.

What, I think, made this truly a work of God is how a nation, filled with people who do not enjoy the communion of the mind, was able to decimate the armies of Israel. God's hand cannot be missed in this instance. Even the rise of Assyria and Babylon was a great feat. Because for a single king to rule such a vast amount of land with such a vast population he must have been greatly respected.

Especially of note is king Nebuchadnezzar of Babylon. The king who brought the killing stroke to the nation of Israel. He is to be noted for he was recorded, in the Book of Daniel, to have gone mad for seven years before regaining back his throne and proclaiming that all that he now has under his rule was given to him by God[9].

This I think is a special period in history where a non-Jewish king actually gained communion with God and Israel. Thus causing his seven years of madness as he tries to reconcile the sudden influx of noise and information gained through communion. And also explains his proclamation, after recovering and regaining his throne, that the God of Israel is the one responsible for all that he possesses under heaven.

Truly without God's miraculous intervention, these swords of judgement could not have been forged.

---

[9]   King Cyrus of Persia also proclaims a similar thing in Ezra 1:2.

HELLENISATION AS GOD'S SEED

With the fall and subsequent failure of Israel, there is now a need for a new work by God. Israel can no longer be the chosen nation that would draw the other nations to God's glory. Therefore the need for a Messiah, a chosen person who can fulfil the task that Israel failed to accomplish.

However God being God cannot be defeated, he would still work through Israel to bring about this Messiah. Thus the first direct prophecies about this Messiah started with Isaiah who witnessed the fall of the Northern kingdom, signalling the beginnings of the fall of Israel.

As time progressed, after the Assyrian and Babylonian empires, God raised a new king who would bring about the rise of a new empire which would eventually pave the way for the coming of the Messiah. This new king was known as Alexander the Great.

He was a great conqueror empowered by God and blessed with a powerful army that was able to build a vast empire that spanned from Greece, on the European continent in the west, to the former Babylonian empire in the east and also spanning southwards all the way to Egypt.

Alexander did not only form a super empire but also created a language and culture that superseded all that was originally present in the nations that were conquered. This phenomenon was known as Hellenisation where the Greek language and culture permeated all the lands that Alexander conquered.

The attraction for it was supposedly because of the openness of Greek logic, philosophy and arts which allowed them to be easily assimilated into the culture of the conquered lands. Thus creating a vast empire where all spoke a common language and had a common mind, related by Greek thought.

This was what planted the seed that would eventually become the even larger Roman Empire that Christ the Messiah entered when he arrived upon this earth. Making it easier for the message of Christ to spread since all in the Roman Empire understood a common language and understood Greek thought.[10]

---

[10] Note that after The Great Schism and Babel, Man is separated not only by a fractured mind but also by different languages. It is because of Hellenisation that these challenges could be surmounted when Christ arrived.

THE MESSIAH

Thus it was in the midst of the Roman Empire that Christ the Messiah came. Glory and hallelujah to God in the highest.

Yet he came, born in a simple stable and brought up as a humble carpenter's son. However, despite this, his arrival had a two-fold purpose. The first was to fulfil Man's need of someone to lead them, a king of kings and a lord of lords. This is seen in the scene when the wise men from the east came to visit baby child Jesus, having heard of the prophecy in their distant lands. Even in the distant lands of the east has God prepared for Christ's glory to be exalted.

Juxtaposing this is the second purpose which is God's need of a saviour for Man. A saviour that can remove away the corruption of Sin. This is Christ's Raison D'etre. To be a man of peace. His blessing to Man and also his personal curse. For in order to fulfil this second purpose, Jesus would eventually be crucified, rather than to reveal his divine and kingly nature during his trial in Jerusalem.

For to reveal his true nature by exercising his divine powers, during his trial, would result in a polarisation of society. Especially between the Jews and the rest of the Roman Empire since all the Jews would then acknowledge the all powerful Jesus as their King and, because of the political situation, would then lead to a Jewish uprising against the Romans.[11] This was not what the peace loving Jesus had in mind.[12]

Only when the cup of God's wrath is full will Jesus exercise his powers of divine judgement. This will come only during the closing of the age. Marked out by signs and portents which are recorded, cryptically, in the Book of Revelations or also known as one of the letters of John the Apostle.

---

[11] A fearsome force would Israel be as they would be able to fight as one large unit through communion of their minds. In addition, Christ's divine powers, that grant him control over all of creation would render Israel invincible.

[12] Note that even John the Baptist was confused about the purpose of Christ for he said, in Matthew 3: 11-12, that Christ would baptise them with fire. Burning the chaff, or the useless troublemakers, with unquenchable fire which is a picture of judgement. Yet we know that even till Christ died and ascended, this did not happen. Even stranger was how Christ often preached about peace, love, repentance and forgiveness while heralding the coming of the Kingdom of Heaven.

SCANDAL OF THE PHARISEES

The Pharisees were an elite group of Jews in Jewish society during the Roman Empire. Those in Jerusalem were the most influential as they were close to the chief priest of the Jewish Temple in Jerusalem. They were the authority over how Jewish Scripture and the Law should be interpreted and executed. Thus they were the spiritual leaders and the judges of Jewish society.

Even Herod who ruled over the Jews had to acquiesce to the advise and proclamations of the Pharisees whenever matters had any relation to Scripture and Jewish Law which is simply almost every matter. Therefore true power laid in the hands of the Pharisees not Herod where many of those in power were Reds.

This was the reason why Jesus always chastised the Pharisees in his teachings, sometimes directly and many a times indirectly for he wishes to expose their folly and hubris. Especially their impracticality in the management of Law and Scripture in Jewish society and also their animosity towards Roman culture and rule.

This was also the reason why Christ refused to proclaim himself as king during his trial in Jerusalem for the Pharisees had laid a political trap to entrap Jesus. The trap was laid after Jesus rode into the town of Jerusalem upon a donkey with the people proclaiming him as the Son of David, king of the Jews. For Jesus had proven his divine identity through the resurrection of Lazarus just before his entry into Jerusalem.

The Pharisees then reported to Pontius Pilate that Jesus was a rebel who wanted to proclaim himself king so as to overthrow the Roman government[13] while to Herod they had Jesus indicted to be a religious charlatan who had no true divine authority. Thus when Jesus was sent from Pontius Pilate to Herod, Herod released Jesus after seeing him as Jesus was deemed to be not a threat to his throne. For Jesus had chosen not to refute any of the claims made by the Pharisees.

Then finally Jesus was brought back to Pontius Pilate on charges of being a blasphemer and it was on that charge the Pharisees wished to see Jesus crucified. Pontius Pilate knowing that he was going to have a Jewish revolt in his hands if he did not quell the raging Jews, who now think Jesus to be a charlatan and blasphemer, decided to flog Jesus before releasing him since Pontius also saw no wrong with Jesus.

But the Pharisees who had the power to preside over Jewish Law continued to press for Jesus to be crucified and Pontius had to eventually relent in order to avoid further social unrest.

Yet throughout this whole scandal, Jesus fulfilled prophecy by playing the innocent lamb that was to be sent for slaughter. Jesus strangely also had no other choice, for to reveal his divine powers and have himself proclaimed king to the authorities in Jerusalem would result in a Roman Jewish war under his leadership. For the Jews would all stand united in proclaiming Jesus as king.

---

[13] Note that when Pontius Pilate sought a private audience with Jesus, during his first meeting with Jesus, away from the angry Jewish crowd. Jesus strangely did nothing to refute the accusations brought against him. But Pontius still chose to release Jesus to the Jews who subsequently brought him to Herod under the charge of blasphemy.

THE SCANDAL OF PENTECOST

Following Jesus's ascension, was the miraculous day of Pentecost where the Holy Spirit descended upon believers in Jesus Christ. This enabled believers to perform various miracles like healing, exorcism and even the speaking of foreign languages.

However what was not known about Pentecost was that it ushered in a new era of Gentile believers who can now also enter into communion with Jews and God upon believing in Jesus. Thus upon their entry into communion came also the ability, of those they commune with, to be able to speak in the foreign tongues of the Gentile believers.

The scandal about all this was that it made the political and social situation in the Roman Empire so much more complicated. The complication arises from the Reds who are part of this communion of the mind among believers. They exist on both sides of the community, among both Jews and Gentiles. And many Pharisees who were formerly the Reds who persecuted Jesus also switched from being non-believers to believers in Christ.

This change was inevitable because of the irrefutable nature of the miracles following Pentecost. But sadly the heart of Man does not change. Even when Man is spiritually cleansed to be able to enter into a spiritual relationship with God and men, evil still exists within the hearts of Man.

So the Pharisees again became the religious leaders after Pentecost, for they were the authority on Scripture and the Law, for even if they could not perform miracles they could speak in tongues which was how they deceived the world into thinking they had spiritual authority.

This was the scandal of Pentecost that led to the complications, that Paul faced, in the Book of Acts.

ANANIAS

The man central to the Scandal of Pentecost is the Temple High Priest, Ananias, who was recorded in Acts to have intended to throw Paul into prison and have him punished under Jewish Law. For Paul was reported to have preached among the Jews and Gentiles to forsake Jewish Law when they believe in Jesus Christ.[14]

High Priest Ananias is also the same disciple who helped Paul regain his sight when he was still named Saul and had been blinded by God.[15] That was the reason why in Acts chapter 22 Paul told the story of Ananias when he stood before the Temple Council of Jerusalem with Ananias the High Priest sitting in.

This was also the reason why the story of a different man with the same name, and a wife called Sapphira, was written in chapter 5 of the Book of Acts. This was to illustrate God's anger and judgement against those who transgress against him and to also illustrate the complication with regard to Ananias the High Priest who strangely was not struck down for being, as Paul puts it, a "whitewashed wall".[16] Meaning Ananias was a hypocrite despite his outward appearance of being a pious follower of the Law.

---

14   Refer to Book of Acts 21-24.
15   Refer to Book of Acts 22: 12-16.
16   Refer to Book of Acts 23: 3.

In short, the Temple of Jerusalem, perceived by many to be the House of the Lord was unclean and corrupted. It was a place where many evil schemes were hatched to gain social and political influence over the people and the Roman government as all who believed in Christ came under the jurisdiction of the Temple.

THE PLOT BETWEEN THE PHARISEES & SADDUCEES[17]

With this new empowered status of the Temple in Jerusalem, as new believers continue to grow in numbers with the spread of the gospel and the miracles that come with it, the influence of the Pharisees grew.

News of the gospel would also eventually reach Rome the seat of power of the Roman Empire. Here Caesar and the Senate oversees this vast Roman Empire. Here is also where Jews like the Sadducees also hold influence and power.

The Reds among the Pharisees and Sadducees who share communion are now able to plot a takeover of the Roman Empire through the rise in Christianity. This would eventually lead to a nightmare engineered by Emperor Nero himself where Christians would be persecuted and the Temple of Jerusalem eventually destroyed.

For no Caesar would allow the grand Roman Empire to fall into the hands of the Jews who would then destroy the original dream of Rome. A prosperous empire with an open multi-cultural society united by trade and Greek thought.

---

[17] Note that there is one stark difference between Pharisees and Sadducees even though both are Jews. The earlier has a strong dislike for the Roman way of life and practice a very inward looking form of Judaism. While the latter is more willing to cooperate and integrate into the Roman way of life and practices a more outward looking form of Judaism.

Furthermore the conniving Reds among the Pharisees and Sadducees are not to be trusted. To allow them a chance to take power would be disastrous for all who would come under their rule. Even Jesus chastised them while he still lived among men.

Therefore the fall of the Temple in Jerusalem in AD70 was in essence inevitable as these events were also foretold by Jesus in Luke 21: 5-9.

A New Order in the Book of Hebrews

With the eradication of the Temple of Jerusalem comes the destruction of its centrality in Jewish and Christian life. The power of the Pharisees and Sadducees were broken. A new order in Christianity now unfolds, where the Jewish authoritative voice over scripture decreases while the authoritative voice of Gentiles increase.

A new order of Faith superseding Law also now arises. Thus culminating in the authoring of the Book of Hebrews that states that Jesus is now our eternal High Priest in the indestructible Temple in Heaven. That it is only by Faith in Jesus that we have our salvation. The old traditions of Jewish Law now fade away because Jesus is not under the old Levitical order but under the new order of Melchizedek.

Melchizedek was a non-Jewish high priest of God before the Laws were created and whom even Abraham gave a third of his acquired possessions, in return for Melchizedek's blessing. Thus Melchizedek is considered greater than even Abraham the First Patriarch of Israel.

The Book of Hebrews is important not only for the new order it proposes but also for the reassurance it provides to the Jewish community for the lost of their Temple. It is an important text that allows for the Jews to move forward after AD70 so that Jewish culture can continue in the absence of the Temple.

AFTER CONSTANTINE

After numerous years of trials and tribulations Christianity finally became a State religion during the reign of Constantine. He was the first Holy Roman Emperor of Rome. Legends say that he became a believer after seeing a shining Cross in the sky before entering a difficult battle which he eventually won.

It was Constantine who first institutionalised the Christian State. A move which was unprecedented as well as controversial as this contravened his role as Caesar to guard the dream of Rome. This miraculous conversion of the Roman Emperor also caused a wave of change to ripple throughout the Empire. Christianity was now free from persecution and could now be practiced openly without fear of reprisals.

By this time most of the Jews have reverted to a private form of Judaism, that is practiced in the absence of the Temple, in order to avoid Christian persecution by the earlier Roman authorities. Thus the pillars of Christian theology and understanding were now found in the gentile population of the Roman Empire.

This then allowed Church Fathers like Augustine to rise to prominence. Bringing with them a sense of unity within the State Church. This also brought about the canonisation of the Bible to become a common point of reference for religious scripture and discussion.

Yet despite this new injection of life into Christianity there were still problems with it. Most of the learned individuals of Christian theology reside with the elite in society. Its understanding and execution controlled mostly by them and as always Reds exist. Many manipulate scripture to their own advantage to give them a social or political edge in Roman society.

In reality, Roman society was gradually crumbling internally. The dream of Rome as an Empire was growing stale despite the communion shared by those who believe in Christ. This can be observed by the constant invasions by the Goth barbarians who were simply displaced and in search of living space and food. However the Roman authorities desired only to keep these brutes out of the empire.

But as they say a hungry man is an angry man and the Goth's eventually invaded and ransacked the apathetic Roman Empire thus breaking it up into smaller pieces. No longer was the Roman Empire a vast continuous territory.

The Empire was gradually split into Eastern Rome, consisting mainly the Middle Eastern countries, and Western Rome which was made up by mainly European countries. With the land now known as Turkey[18] being the capital of Eastern Rome and Rome in Italy being the capital of Western Rome.

Even as both Eastern and Western Rome remained Christian after Constantine, it was mainly a religion that swayed under the influence of the ruling class. A ruling class that mostly sought ostentatious displays of Rome's wealth and power. The Hagia Sophia being one of such demonstrations under Emperor Justinian.

Christianity was now a far cry from how it first started with Christ. From a religion concerned with the common man and man's communion with God it has become a religion concerned only with power and influence. The common man and his needs has become largely ignored.

Even the Jews preferred their old simple traditions compared to such a form of Christianity.

---

[18] To be exact the capital of Eastern Rome resided mainly in Constantinople, Turkey.

THE PROPHET MUHAMMAD

It is under this atmosphere that Muhammad, later to become the Final Prophet of Islam, came into being. It was under this environment that a new work begun. Seeing the decrepit condition of the Church, Muhammad the outsider who shared no communion in the Church was given revelations and visions while he sought God in a cave.

Muhammad, a common man, was given communion with God and communion with men. The revelations and visions he received became, eventually, what is known today as Islam. Muhammad a son of Abraham through the line of Ishmael now joins in communion with Jews and Christians.

A new word has been given to Muhammad which would spread throughout the Middle East. With the decline in Christianity this new word of God from the mouth of a common man would take root in the hearts of many. Soon much of Eastern Rome would soon be converted to Islam. A religion that recognises God as one and the brotherhood of Man under one God.

Muhammad though sharing communion was given a new path but even in the midst of this new path he continued to show reverence for the Jews who also share the same bloodline as him through Abraham. Christians were also tolerated for they worship the God of Abraham as well.[19]

---

19   Bruce Feiler is an author who wrote a books titled "Walking the Bible" and "Abraham: A Journey to the Heart of Three Faiths" where in his interactions with various people of the Biblical Lands, Jews, Christians and Arabs, realises how much of shared heritage the people of these Lands have. A heritage that should bond them as fellow brothers, for first and foremost, they are all sons of Abraham and all worship the God that Abraham worshiped.

This new light in the East overshadowed the dream of Rome and Christianity and spread like wild fire. With new believers also coming to share in communion with Jews and Christians. Eventually becoming a new nation in the midst of the Eastern Roman Empire. A new balance of power has been forged in Eastern Rome, shared between Islam and Christianity.

BLACK DEATH & THE WESTERN DARK AGES

During Emperor Justinian's reign in Eastern Rome Black Death or The Plague became the scourge of Western Rome. Hypothesized to have been brought about by rats on ships traversing from Eastern Rome to Western Rome, with people living in Eastern Rome being resistant to it, since they have been living with it for years.

It is believed that the barbarian invasions, that ransacked Western Rome, together with the bubonic plague, Black Death, led to the rapid deterioration of Western Rome. Governance and civilization in Western Rome collapsed with the massive division and deaths that were wrought by the two scourges.

This then led to the Western Dark Ages, where culture and learning almost ceased to exist. Roads were not maintained and towns lost connection with one another for fear of catching the plague. It was only later that brave souls, who would be known as monks, would rise to save whatever learning and literature that could be found by copying them onto scrolls for posterity.

Monk strongholds that were self-sustaining started to pop up providing refuge to those who require it.

EMERGING FROM THE DARKNESS

And the whole of Western Rome which essentially was Europe was to remain in the Dark Ages for two to three hundred years before it showed signs of recovery. By then Europe was shared between the former inhabitants of Western Rome and the barbarians who had invaded. Christianity of a rather primitive and superstitious form was practiced generally.

The first significant leader to emerge and unite a portion of Europe would be Charles Martel "The Hammer". He was a brilliant military leader and strategist who united the Franks. Under his leadership he drove back the Muslim Turks who had managed to conquer their way into Europe although it was only through Charlemagne his grandson that the Turks were completely driven out of Europe.

It was also under Charlemagne that most of Western Europe finally became united under him as the Holy Roman Emperor. With Charlemagne's christening, "Western Rome" which is also now known as the Western Church, has now been resurrected.

This resurrection then led to the development of medieval Europe while a delicate balance of power was maintained in "Eastern Rome" also now known as the Eastern Orthodox Church. It is this bi-polar development of the Western and Eastern Churches that would later lead to the crusades.[20]

---

[20] The development of the two churches were very different. For the Western Church its seat of authority lies with the Pope who resides in Rome. The Pope together with several medieval kings governed Europe. But the Eastern Church had no central Pope and was united under one king.

THE CRUSADES

The Crusades was essentially a battle over religious ideology. Despite the communion that was shared by the Jews, Christians and Muslims, the authorities residing within the Western and Eastern Churches decided that Christianity would be the one to reign supreme and it would be achieved by warfare.

This event would be triggered by a letter from the king of the Eastern Church to the Pope in Western Rome. The letter would request for the assistance of the Pope to gather a force to reclaim the "Holy Lands of the Christians". The Pope would then declare a Holy war upon the infidel Muslims and make an official declaration to all of Europe that those who take part in this Holy struggle would be granted a pardon from God for their sins and be assured entry into paradise upon death.

The religious thrust of the Pope's message was powerful. For the argument that Christianity is the true religion as it acknowledges Christ while the others were heresy was, in some sense, undeniable. For in time to come, the crusaders would not only see to the death of Muslims but Jews as well. All who do not acknowledge Christ would die by the sword. Conversion would be acquired by force.

The Crusades was also in some sense a battle for the dictates of truth. That the truth of Christ be acknowledged by all. However the irony is would Christ the peacemaker, even to the point of being crucified, have approved of this conflict?

THE WESTERN CHURCH
AND CONFLICT[21]

Apart from the Crusades, which eventually died out, after about two hundred years, as the Western Church finally realised that it was not going to succeed as the Muslims continued to push back the advances of the Crusaders, the Church was also involved in many other forms of conflict that include the territorial and political feuds of Europe and also the Inquisition.

Europe after Charlemagne was always embroiled in dispute that was territorial and political in nature. Ironically when it came to the Crusades many would stand united but otherwise the authorities in power would be squabbling over various issues and fighting over them.

While the Western Church, whose seat of power was in Rome, would oversee these squabbles seeking to find a balance of power which more often than not is a balance that would also serve its own interests. Alliances and pacts were made and broken in this constant struggle for influence and power over the dictates of good and evil.

---

[21] The Eastern Church developed very differently once it extricated itself from being involved with the Crusades. It had no central authority like the Pope of the Western Church and gradually spread into Russia mainly though the efforts of monks and clergy. The conflicts that do erupt in the Eastern Church were mainly feudal disputes which generally did not involve matters of religion.

The Protestant Reformation

The power that the Church wields over the kingdoms in Europe is undeniable. It has many eyes, ears and mouths inserted into every circle of power and authority. Its will and voice would be made known as and when it wants to. Yet not everyone was agreeable with how the Church handled its affairs, including those within the Church itself.

Eventually a member of the Church did stand up to question the Church's hegemonic legitimacy and this man is known as Martin Luther. A man who dared question the Church and its practices which later led to a significant event in history that is known as "The Protestant Reformation".

Martin Luther supposedly nails several papers to a church door and each paper questions certain Church practices and beliefs. An example of one of the practices that was questioned was the practice of indulgences where the Church would prescribe a sum of money, for a man, to be paid in propitiation of certain sins. Once paid the Church would then grant an official pardon to the man which also meant that the man no longer needed to stand trial for the wrongdoings that were pardoned.

Basically the practices and beliefs that were brought into question were the ones which grant the Church hegemonic control over the population of Europe. Especially since control over the interpretation of scripture was solely in the hands of the Church authorities in Rome. Therefore, to put it rather bluntly, a bad Pope[22] and his lackeys would have unprecedented control over Europe.

Thus what the Protestant Reformation sought to achieve is to protest against Church monopoly over the lives of the people through scripture. It also sought to decentralise the interpretation of scripture by placing it into the hands of common men and this was achievable because of the prior invention of the Gutenberg Printing Press. This then allowed for the mass production of the Bible, like the Gutenberg Bible, for the common masses.

Ownership over what scripture meant became more personal as people began to own their own Bibles. Certain Kingdoms like Britain also began to break away from the hegemony of the Western Church. Kings can now also claim ownership over the interpretation of scripture.

---

[22] Note that this is not a comment that all Popes are bad power hungry wolves in sheep clothing. There exist Popes who are well-meaning in the midst of the politics of Europe.

1603 - King James of the United Kingdom

One such king was James I of the United Kingdom which was the first time in history that the three kingdoms of the British Isles consisting of Scotland, England and Ireland were united under one king. He broke away from Church hegemony and even instituted his own version of the Bible also known as the King James Bible.

He even proceeded to write several books which established the divine unction of kings thus justifying the authority of kings over scripture and state.[23] His purpose was to justify the existence of kingdoms being independent of Church Papacy and to establish, from a Godly perspective, their rule of law.

In some sense, he had merely transferred the Church's ruling sceptre into his own hands thus allowing him to hold both the sceptres of Kingdom and Church and giving him more power and influence. However what he did was also a reformation of sorts, proving that dependence on the central Church can be broken. This, he was able to achieve, because of a twist of fate. For he was fated, as King James VI of Scotland, to be next in line to inherit the throne of England, that was already united with Ireland, when Queen Elizabeth died. For his mother was the half-sister of Queen Elizabeth.

---

[23] Examples of such books that were authored by King James I are "Daemonologie", "True Law of Free Monarchies" and "Basilikon Doron".

Not to mention the geographical separation of the British Isles from the main European continent also made it easier for King James to enforce his independence. It was a confluence of many factors which eventually allowed a kingdom to "reform" and break away from the hegemony of the Western Church. Thus forming one of the first protestant churches, a Christian community that was independent of oversight from the Western Catholic Papacy in Rome.

This then gradually paved the way for a more personal and private form of Christianity.

The Pilgrim Fathers
of North America

A new form of Christianity was emerging, one that would be even further decentralised. A form of Christianity, where despite the communion shared by all believers, can be composed of just a family of believers with the Father as the head of the small "church".

This was achieved in the New World of America, a continent made famous by Christopher Columbus's discovery. More accurately it was in North America that this new form of Christianity came about. Brought about by the English Pilgrim Fathers who were seeking independence from the Church of England during the reign of King James I, supported by private investors under the pretext of colonising the New World.

This was what herald the birth of North America, subsequently known as the United States of America (USA).

Learning to live with differences - The First Amendment

The history of USA was a tumultuous one. Its beginning was a War of Independence from the British. However the time leading to its formation allowed for many localise churches to spring up. Each having its own flavour of interpretation of the Bible. This being independent of any centralised Church control.

Yet during the War of Independence all natively born Americans joined up together despite their religious differences to fight for their independence from British rule. And when they had succeeded the new nation that was formed included a very important ingredient into their constitution which was "The First Amendment".

This significant piece of the constitution allowed for the formation of an entirely secular government that was not guided on religious grounds such that no particular form of religion would be able to establish laws or governments to its benefit.

This effectively then allowed for the freedom to practice any form of religion without persecution or inquisition. Thus the Christians of USA would now have to learn to live with their differences in opinions with regard to interpretations of the Bible. Christianity has now become more personal and private than communal.

The conflicts that Original Sin brought about prior to the Fall of Man as a result of differences in dictates of what is right or wrong now have to be appeased and relinquished under the First Amendment. Every man is free to practice his own brand of religion.

USA, a supposed land of freedom, individuality, opportunity and dreams has been created.[24]

_____

24 Though at some points it was at the cost of the Native Indians who live in the land.

THE GREATEST IRONY - THE CRUCIBLE OF WAR[25] & THE CYCLES OF HISTORY AND PROPHECIES

The Crucible of War is also The Crucible of Conflict. Its inauguration being the day Man partook of the fruit from the Tree of Knowledge of Good & Evil. It is in this Crucible that lives and history are forged, tested and refined. The irony of it is that God intended Paradise to be harmonious in the beginning but with the death and resurrection of Christ clearing away Man's Sin, Man need no longer be burdened by the guilt and shame brought about by conflict which is Original Sin.

No temptation has overtaken you that is not common to man. God is faithful, and he will not let you be tempted beyond your ability, but with the temptation he will also provide the way of escape, that you may be able to endure it. 1 Corinthians 10:13 (ESV)

---

[25] "Crucible of War" is also a reference to a book titled "Crucible of War: The Seven Years' War and the Fate of Empire in British North America, 1754 - 1766", written by Fred Anderson. It is a book on the events leading up to the American Revolutionary War of Independence. How it was essentially a rebellion against the British Manifest Destiny of Empire and its hollowness when placed beside its Christian Ideals where men are considered equals in Christ. Worth a look on Google for in it lies an irony of modern day America when placed beside its modern day economic and political imperialism. Another more archaic but well-known text that touches on the same irony is "Gunga Din" a poem by Rudyard Kipling.

God has devised a way out through the use of Sin which imperfect men will never be able to avoid. The Crucible of Conflict is now the tool which God uses to forge, test and refine Man. And through Christ, Man would no longer be stained by the Sin of conflict.

It is in conflict that heroes or villains are forged. For it is in conflict and what comes after, that a man's true intentions surface and it is in conflict that men are refined, showing grit, courage and valour or reel in shame and repentance for the wrongs they have done. History itself is also forged in its Crucible written through cycles of conflict, tested by its outcomes and refined through the lessons that come out of it.

Even prophecies are mostly fulfilled in its Crucible as they are mostly about the rise and fall of men and his kingdoms or nations arising from conflict.[26] The Wheel of Time or the Cycles of History and Prophecy all involve conflict. It is as if God or the powers that be foresee all human events as being driven by conflict and the only way to break the prophecies is to take away conflict. In the words of Robert Jordan, author of the "Wheel of Time" series, *the Dark One seeks to break the Wheel* but the irony is that to do that one has to remove conflict not cause it.

It is as if God has entrapped the Devil and this is possible only because the Devil is too predictable. God is able to foresee many steps ahead of the Devil and shift events to fit His perfect will. So no matter how bad things become the Devil can never out manoeuvre God.

Therefore all the conflict in the Western Church, Eastern Church before the formation of America or after its formation all serve God's purpose. Even the tumultuous history of USA before and after its formation serves its purpose. For when Judgement day comes, the conflict that everyman has gone through will serve to bring out his true self to the surface for lives are forged, tested and refined through its Crucible.

---

[26] Refer to - Abraham, David, Isaiah, Ezekiel, Jeremiah, Revelations; Greek stories about Hercules, Perseid, Child of Cronus, Bellerophoniad; Ragnarok in the Nordic Poetic Edda & Prose Edda, Islamic End Times. Most texts with prophetic elements almost always involve some form of conflict.

In the words of Master Sergeant Farell of the movie "Edge of Tomorrow" - *Battle is the Great Redeemer. It is the Fiery Crucible in which true heroes are forged. The one place where all men truly share the same rank, regardless of what kind of parasitic scum they were [before] going in.*

EPILOGUE - REALITY, OUT OF THE RABBIT HOLE[27]

What does it all mean? It means that the Devil has been in the details all along. Ever since the forbidden fruit was ingested, the Devil has always sought to disrupt the harmony in God's creation. The many battles that have been fought, throughout history, are a testament to this fact.

Therefore at the end of the day what Jesus was trying to teach is not just about peace and love but ultimately how conflict can be resolved. For Jesus, in reality, did not abstain from conflict for he heavily criticized the Pharisees and Sadducees but yet, at the end of his time on earth, he chose to avoid a physical massacre by allowing himself to be persecuted and crucified. Yet this does not provide a complete perspective as it does not answer the necessity of war unless one dives into the Old Testament.

This means that Christian theology is riddled with fallacies. Because God is not just a God of peace but a God of War, among many other things as well. These diametrically opposite faces of God cannot be accounted for in a theology that is just about peace and love. And even if a theology of righteous conflict is created out of the stories of the Old Testament, before Christ, how confident can Christians be that the Devil is not in the details.

At the end of the day, when one takes a bird's eye view of history, the unavoidable conclusion is that conflict is inevitable and sometimes even

---

[27] "Out of the rabbit hole" is a reference from Lewis Carrol's "Alice's Adventures in Wonderland".

necessary. The main reason for this being, there will always be differences. People or groups of people with opposing views will always exist.

And if God does not only desire harmony but that all Man turn his eyes to acknowledge Him as God then woe it is to Man for many will fall away. Pushed away by the numerous conflicts in history involving the Monotheistic religions. Even until today this conflict continues in the Middle East.

These are the reasons why I am compelled to write and also why, to believe in them, leads to the worse of outcomes. For statistically[28], nearly half of the world's population does not believe in the God of Abraham. While among the other half that believe, Christianity forms about a third of the world, Islam is about a fifth and Judaism constitutes less than one percent of the world's population. If you work out the maths heaven is going to be a crummy place, for whichever religion is right, as most of the others would be theoretically be thrown into hell.

The worst thing is that people are thrown into hell for reasons which are not of their own doing. Simply put, *it is not their fault.*

It is not their fault that the Middle East is in conflict. It is not their fault that Jerusalem which means "Foundation of Harmony" is no longer a beacon for the God of Abraham but a symbol of oppression toward Muslims in the Gaza. It is also not their fault that the history of the Church is filled with violence from wars and inquisition.

How then can the world be saved if it is pivoted on the belief in God let alone Jesus Christ?

*****

---

[28]   Based on the published statistics of the CIA's online World Factbook, which can be found on Wikipedia as well by searching for "religion statistics".

Radicalisation is when one has an extreme unfounded righteous prejudice. Therefore there is a very thin line between a just combatant and a radical combatant because both think they are right. One man's perception of justice might be perceived by another as radical.

Thus always be wary when ones beliefs require one to take a combative stance as it may be perceived as a form of radicalisation.